The Journey

By

Jim Sano

Full Quiver Publishing
Pakenham ON

This book is a work of fiction.
The characters and incidents are products of the author's imagination.

The Journey
copyright 2024
by James G. Sano
ISBN 978-1-987970-69-2

Published by Full Quiver Publishing
PO Box 244
Pakenham, Ontario K0A 2X0

Printed and bound in the USA

Cover illustration copyright, Bob Biedrzycki. Used with permission.
Cover design by Jim Sano

NATIONAL LIBRARY OF CANADA
CATALOGUING IN PUBLICATION

Published by FQ Publishing
A Division of Innate Productions

Dedication

The Journey is dedicated to all the young readers who love reading stories, going on adventures, and imagining themselves and the characters facing new challenges. I especially want to dedicate this book to Mariella Nielsen and Gavin Ryan, who graciously offered to read an early draft and provide their insightful and helpful feedback. Thank you.

Books by Jim Sano

The Father's Son

Gus Busbi

Stolen Blessing

Van Horn

Self-Portrait

Fallen Graces

The Journey

Chapter 1

Thirteen-year-old Will Donovan stood immobilized as he stared at the unfinished attic wall in front of him. A bare light bulb hung behind, casting his shadow on the old wooden slats. His shadow, taller and more formidable than he, wore high boots, a wide-brimmed hat with a feather plume, a draped short coat, and a sword at his side. While Will trembled somewhere deep inside, his shadow did not. But maybe his shadow didn't realize that he stood on the threshold between the life he knew and the completely unknown. Could he do this?

Will braced himself. He had to do this.

As much as he longed to start the day over, he could not. This morning had begun like many others as he sat at the kitchen table, eating scrambled eggs and a warm waffle covered in golden buttermilk syrup.

"Sam," called his mother, "you're going to be late for school again!"

"He's never going to make it. Why do we keep babying him?" asked Will.

Mom turned away from the sink, tucked a curly lock of hair behind her ear, and gave Will a stern look. "If he misses that bus, you'll just have to walk him to school."

"Ma, he's late, he's slow, and he asks too many questions," Will blurted, dropping his fork onto his plate. "Does he have to walk with me? He's ten years old now. It's embarrassing." Will shook his head and pushed away from the table. He liked to be on time for things, but Sam always dragged his feet, his mind everywhere but on what he should've been doing, and going on and on with questions while they meandered to school.

"William Donovan III, you can't always be thinking of

yourself. He's your younger brother, and you know I barely make it to work on time after getting breakfast and such ready for you two."

Mom worked hard, and he regretted complaining. Dad had left them ten years ago, disappearing without a note or explanation. Maybe he'd just been restless, but he'd left Mom pregnant and with a three-year-old boy and no money to get by.

Will's grandfather, Bill "Poppie" Donovan, gave them the family's old Victorian house and helped Mom find a job at the manufacturing plant in town to support herself and the boys. Poppie visited often. He was the only male mentor they had. *How different would these hurried days be with Dad at home?*

As Will brought his dish to the sink, Sam came scrambling down the old wooden stairs and stood outside the kitchen doorway, his floppy brown hair uncombed, one side of his shirt untucked, and wearing two different colored socks. "See, I'm ready! I won't be late!"

He rolled his eyes as Mom said, "Make sure you eat some of that breakfast."

Picking up his backpack, Will headed to the door as Sam grabbed a waffle off the plate, kissed Mom, and sprinted to catch up. Will was already ten steps ahead of him down the sidewalk. By the time they reached the front of Sam's old one-story school, Will had pushed Sam's hair down, tucked in his shirt, and pulled his trouser legs down to hide his mismatched socks.

"Have a good day, Will!" yelled Sam as he scurried to the front door of his school.

Just ahead on the leaf-covered sidewalk approached Will's two best friends. He called Isaac Porter "Porty," partly because of his last name but also because he was large and heavy. Porty was also funny and good-hearted. Will called his other best friend, Arthur Braggle, "Arrie." The taller, dark-haired Arrie could be serious, self-focused, and hot-tempered, but he was a loyal and committed friend. Arrie wore glasses that looked more like goggles to Will.

"Hey, are we all set for tonight?" A big smile stretched across Porty's freckled face as he shoved his red bangs off his forehead.

For the past few months, Will and his friends had devoted themselves to making the best Halloween costumes ever. Nothing could stop The Three Musketeers. They'd labored over every detail, making their costumes as authentic as possible—at least from what they'd gathered from the historical adventure novel by Alexandre Dumas they'd read in class.

A voice echoed from behind as they neared the school's front entrance. "Are you boys ready for a swashbuckling adventure tonight?"

They turned to see Jules Cappello standing with a twinkle in her eyes and a smile on her face. Jules had played with the boys for years and had been just as good at baseball and basketball as any of them. Standing before them now in a blue dress and white sweater, she looked more like a girl than the tomboy they had grown up with.

"Hey, Jules," said Arrie as the girl glanced toward Will.

Porty stepped back, pretending to draw a sword from the imaginary scabbard at his hip. He then flashed it back and forth in front of her. "The Three Musketeers are always ready! We never fear quarrels but seek hazardous adventures!"

Arrie and Will stepped back, drew their imaginary swords, and held them high to one another. In unison, they exclaimed, "All for one, and one for all, for it is united we stand and divided we fall!"

Jules held her hands to her lips and bent over in laughter. "I love it, and I'm glad you three finally found a book to capture your interest. Off you go, and good luck on your adventure, for 'the merit of all things lies in their difficulty!'"

Porty turned to Will and Arrie, eyebrows raised. "Is that in the story? I hope it's not on the test today."

After school, Porty and Arrie came home with Will to finish their costumes and map out the game plan for their Halloween route. Mom never minded the extra company. In fact, she enjoyed the lively conversation over dinner, especially on a night like Halloween. "I'm sure you four boys will bring back more candy than you can eat before next year's trick-or-treating."

Will crossed his arms and turned to Mom. "Four? We're The Three Musketeers."

"Well, you'll be three musketeers and a mummy tonight."

Will's head dropped back as he rolled his eyes and pleaded silently with the ceiling. "Mom. Why does Sam need to come with us?" he said, ignoring Sam, who sat right next to him at the dining room table.

"Because his friends live across town, and you are his brother." His mother gazed into Will's eyes. "Will, you'll understand this more later; we have a responsibility to care about others, especially as an older brother. You're going to have to trust me on this."

He recoiled at the appeal to trust, the very word

causing him to wince. He may have wanted the right to be selfish once in a while, or maybe he was angry about his father, but the sight of his brother's imploring expression brought him out of his thoughts.

After dinner, the dishes washed and put away, Mom stood Sam up. She tilted her head, looking him over with a roll of ace bandages in one hand. "Will, you turn him slowly as I wrap."

Sam patiently twirled around while Mom wrapped his torso, legs, and head in bandages, leaving narrow openings for his eyes and mouth.

"Hey, Will, if you really don't want me around, I can walk a little bit in front of you," said Sam in a muffled voice as the bandages slipped over his mouth.

"Fine. Just don't embarrass me. That's all I ask," Will snapped. His conscience bothered him a little, but he still didn't want Sam attached to him all night.

"Will! That's your brother." Mom leaned toward Will and whispered, "Don't you know how much he looks up to you? How would you feel if you had no friends to go with when you were ten? Can you just do this for Sam—for me?"

Will sighed, patted his brother on the head, and went up to his room with Porty and Arrie to put on their musketeer outfits and practice their swordplay.

Ten minutes later, Will stood on his bed, battling the other two musketeers, and then spotted another figure dressed as a musketeer in the doorway.

The door opened and he stopped mid-swing. "What are you doing here?"

Jules strode confidently into the room and drew her sword. She wore a wide-brimmed feathered musketeer hat, an ivory shirt with puffy long sleeves and ruffles, a tunic with the image of a cross, black leather gloves, and tall boots. "Haven't you guys been reading the book? D'Artagnan was the fourth musketeer. You can't go out without me."

Will jumped down with a loud thump. "Great. We have The Three Musketeers, a midget mummy, and now a cross-dressing female musketress. This was not the plan."

Jules whisked the tip of her sword to the underside of Will's chin. "Sometimes you have to go with the flow—plus, I have the long hair to look like an authentic musketeer!" Jules typically wore her auburn hair in a ponytail, and none of the boys had ever seen it down.

Arrie pushed up his flowing sleeves and rubbed his chin. "She does have a point there—and she's got the best costume too."

Porty nodded.

Giving in, Will shook his head and clunked down the wooden stairs in his boots, followed by the rest of the troop. They assembled by the front door, ready to go.

Mom stood smiling as she gazed at Will, Jules, Porty, and Arrie in their musketeer costumes next to Sam, the mummy, ready to fill the pillow sacks they held. "Wait, let me get a picture."

After three hours of warning of tricks but receiving treats, the five arrived home ready to collapse and count their loot. This task needed to be done in the privacy of the attic room on the third floor, an old space where they had played, told stories, and created a bond of friendship over many years. With their bags of loot in hand, they climbed the steps to the unfinished but intimate nineteenth-century Victorian attic. A hanging light bulb shone on a thread-bare braided round rug they'd once found, but the light didn't reach the dark, creepy corners filled with old boxes and wobbly wooden chairs covered in spiderwebs. Will had always looked forward to rainy afternoons as an excuse to play here.

Excitement building, Will picked out a spot on the rug, and everyone emptied their pillowcases, creating a treasure trove of candy on the floor. Will began sorting and counting when a knock sounded on the door. He got up and opened it a crack. Sam, who had become half-unraveled during the night, stood on the other side of the door, peering up at Will through sad brown eyes, his pillowcase bulging with candy clasped in one hand. Will sighed and opened the door wide to let him in.

While Will and his friends sorted their candy into piles, Sam sat on an old comforter and popped Skittles and Swedish Fish into his mouth. His gaze kept traveling to the attic's corners and the stacks of old boxes of unknown treasures. After a while, Sam seemed to have worked up some courage. He got up and shuffled to the darkest corner.

"What's this?" Sam said, his voice muffled. He stepped back into the light with an old pouch dangling from his hand by a leather strap. Eyes open wide as if he'd stumbled upon his very own mystery, he clomped toward Will and stepped on Will's largest candy bar. "Oops," he said, glancing down at the crushed candy.

Will grabbed the pouch and yelled, "Sam! Look what you did! Why do I put up with you?"

"I'm sorry, Will. I didn't see it."

Still irritated, Will opened the pouch and plunged his hand inside. His fingers bumped something metal. He grabbed what felt like a handle and slowly lifted the object—an old pewter piece resembling a trophy cup or goblet with two ornate handles curled into serpent heads. A beaded pattern circled the brim, and various plants and creatures he didn't recognize decorated the bowl.

Sam reached for the goblet. "I found it!"

Will pulled it away before Sam could touch it.

"It's mine! Why do you get everything?" yelled Sam.

Will held it above his head. "What? I get everything, huh? All I do is take care of you. I can't have time with my friends without you tagging along and ruining things. I wish you would just leave me alone and disappear!"

Sam's mouth fell open, and his eyebrows drew together. His eyes turned glossy as he gazed up at Will, but he gave no reply. Then, a tear escaped and trickled down his cheek.

The breath left Will's chest. If only he could take back his words. He shouldn't have—shouldn't have said that. The pain in Sam's eyes sent a knife through Will's heart. Wanting to undo it somehow, he reached out for Sam.

Sam avoided his touch and turned away. Then he ran toward the back wall and vanished into the shadows.

"Sam?" Will tilted the dangling bare lightbulb, shining light into the dark corners, revealing boxes and more boxes, but no Sam.

Jules came up beside Will. "Where did he go?"

"I-I don't know." He shined the light here, there, and everywhere, panic creeping into his chest. "Sam!"

Arrie and Porty searched each wall, corner, and box. No Sam.

Will twisted toward the attic door. It was still shut tight. Panic filled his chest. "Sam, this isn't funny anymore. Come out!"

Suddenly, a faint rapping at the attic door made him

jump. With a deep sigh of relief, he darted toward the closed door and flung it open. But Sam did not stand on the other side.

Chapter 2

"Poppie!" Balancing on the top step, Will forced a broad smile onto his face, attempting to hide his panic as he closed the attic door behind him. "When did you get here?"

Will's grandfather gripped the rail while taking a few deep breaths after climbing the two long flights of stairs. Composing himself, he tugged one side of his old tweed jacket and adjusted his wire-rimmed glasses. His mustache and matching white hair in need of a trim glowed under the old light fixture in the stairwell. The familiar, loving smile faded as his gaze shifted to the pewter goblet in Will's hands. "After all these years playing in the attic, you've found it, have you?"

Will whispered to ensure Mom couldn't hear his words. "It's not this I need to find. Sam was in the attic with us, and now he's gone. He . . . he . . . um . . ."

"Disappeared?" said Poppie with raised eyebrows.

Nodding, Will glanced over his shoulder at the closed door to the attic, then returned his attention to Poppie on the steps.

"Was he near that back wall?"

Will gasped as he gazed into his grandfather's wise blue eyes. "How did you know?"

"Can I see that?" Poppie pointed to the goblet.

Suspecting Poppie knew more about all this, Will handed it to him.

A gleam came to Poppie's eyes as if he marveled at the reappearance of a very old friend. "When you first picked it up, did you happen to notice a number etched in the middle of the goblet?"

"Number?" Will thought and then remembered the

number *10* engraved on it. "Um. It was a ten. Why?"

His grandfather turned the cup toward Will. An ornately scrolled *9* replaced the *10* he'd seen earlier.

"Huh, I could have sworn it was a ten."

"And it was," Poppie replied.

"What do you mean? I can see right there"—he pointed— "it's a nine."

Porty hollered through the closed attic door. "Did you find Sam?"

"Hold on, Porty. Just wait for a second!" Will turned back to Poppie. "Why did you say it *was* a ten?"

Glancing down the stairs, Poppie waved Will back. He reached over and opened the door to the attic. "I have my breath now. Let's go in and talk."

"Poppie, we need to find Sam." Desperation and a bit of guilt washed over Will. "I don't know where he went."

Taking a deep breath, Poppie made his way into the attic, where Will's friends, still in their musketeer outfits, greeted him. "Jules, Porty, Arrie. Can someone tell me if Sam disappeared at *that* back wall?" Poppie pointed to the wall behind them.

"We don't know." Arrie shrugged with open hands. "He was here and ran in that direction; then he was gone. It's dark, but we've looked everywhere up here."

"Three times." Porty held up three stout fingers.

Lifting the goblet, Poppie's bushy eyebrows bounced as if he held a secret.

"What is it?" Jules played with the big feather on her musketeer hat, her eyes wide with curiosity.

Poppie stooped over, moving slowly and wincing a bit, then placed the goblet in the center of the rug under the hanging light. "First, tell me if anyone held this goblet and made a wish."

Jules, Porty, and Arrie turned to Will, the only one to hold the goblet.

Will's brow tightened as he tried to recall the few minutes he had held it. "Um, Sam found the leather pouch. I grabbed it from him when he stepped on my pile of candy. I was upset with him, and he complained that I always got my way or something and—" Will stopped mid-sentence.

His grandfather put his hand on Will's shoulder. "Take your time and try to think of the exact words you used. Don't worry about how they make you feel."

Will shook his head and sank to his knees. "I don't know. Um, I was mad at him. Why was I so mad at him? I think I said something like, 'I wish you'd disappear and leave me alone.' I don't know why I said that, but now he's gone. What happened? Is he okay?"

Poppie reached out and lifted Will from his knees. "Will, panic and fear won't help your brother, nor will guilt. We must focus and have courage if we want to help him."

Will gazed at his grandfather, his mind filling with confusion and fear. "Where is he? What do you know about this?"

"We need to keep this to ourselves. That goblet will grant ten wishes to the one person chosen to use them. Whether you like it or not, you are that person, Will. You unknowingly used one of those wishes when you held it in your hands. The only way to get him back is to go after him."

Arrie scratched his head. "Why can't he just wish him back?"

Will ran his hand through his dark brown hair and looked to his friends for help to wake up from this nightmare. Then he refocused on his grandfather. "How do you know all this?"

Poppie took Will's hand. "Will, you know I grew up in this house and played in this very attic at your age. Well, once, I got into trouble and didn't want to face your great-grandfather, so I came up to the attic. I was rummaging through one of the trunks and found the goblet. While holding it, I heard my father climbing the stairs and wished I could disappear. I ran to that back wall to hide and somehow passed through it."

Will continued to stare at him. "Passed through? Passed through what?"

"That wall is the threshold to another place, another time, and a journey that will test every ounce of courage, determination, and will you have."

Will jerked back, his mind struggling to grasp Poppie's words. He turned toward the shadowy wall. "Me? How can I save him? What's on the other side of that wall?"

Gripping Will's shoulder, Poppie replied, "This journey is yours, should you choose to face it. I can't prepare you for it, and I have no clue what awaits you on the other side, grandson, because it will be different for you than it was for me. But I do know you alone must make the choice."

Trembling now, Will grabbed Poppie's arm. "I-I don't know what I'm choosing. Where will I go? How long is this journey?" He glanced at his friends, a sick feeling making him weak.

Poppie shook his head. "Well, I tell you, on this side of the wall, time will not pass at all. But I do not know how long it will be for you or even what you'll encounter on your journey. I do know this: you'll be tested beyond what you think possible, and once you cross over, there's no turning back. But—"

"But, what?" asked Porty.

Poppie smiled. "But it is an adventure unlike anything you would ever imagine. And as I said, it will require courage and perseverance, but after all, doesn't the merit of all things lie in their difficulty?"

Will turned to catch Jules's smile at the phrase from *The Three Musketeers* she had quoted earlier today.

"Will, only you can make this decision, and only you can save your brother. I'm going down to make sure your mom doesn't worry about the yelling up here. I told her I'd investigate." Poppie took Will by both shoulders and gazed into his eyes. "I have faith in you, Will. You are a Donovan."

Will twisted away. "So was my dad, but he didn't have enough honor or courage to even stay with Mom and us."

Poppie lifted Will's chin and met his gaze. "You can do this. Remember three things. First, always keep the pouch and this goblet with you—and use them prudently. They are vital. Second, be willing to let go and trust completely in the good, and don't be deceived by what you know is not true. You must follow your heart and not your ego. Third, know that I love you and believe in you. Don't ever forget that." Poppie gave Will a long, firm hug and then opened the door, ready to descend the stairs to the first floor, where Mom was probably anxiously waiting for an explanation.

Will trembled as he turned toward the back wall. It was nothing but old wooden boards, but he trusted his grandfather more than anyone in the world—plus, he had to find Sam. His brother was gone, and it was his fault and his responsibility alone to save him. He breathed in deeply and exhaled to calm his paralyzing fear and the overwhelming resistance inside. He was a boy, not a man.

What could he do? Will picked up the goblet and placed it in the pouch, only to hear a small, unfamiliar voice.

"Watch what you're doing."

Will held the pouch in front of him and opened the flap, spotting some movement as he peered in. He held the opening toward the light and shook his head, struggling to believe his eyes.

Porty shuffled closer. "What is it?"

The small voice responded, "I'm not an 'it,' Mr. Porter."

Will set down the bag, and he and his friends gathered around to see a tiny creature, no more than six inches high, staring up with his hands on his hips.

"Are you just going to leave me in here after all these years hanging on that hook?"

Jules grinned as Will gently lifted him from the pouch and set him down. He looked like a tiny elf with light greenish skin, pointed ears, and a large nose. He wore a brown tunic, a tie, boots, and a hat made of leather.

"How did you know my name?" asked Porty.

"Who are you?" Will crossed his arms over his chest.

"I thought you'd never ask. My name is Stitch, and you are William Donovan III if I'm not mistaken. I believe these are your comrades and mates, Jules, Arrie, and Porty. Do I have that right?"

"How do you know so much?" Arrie dropped down to one knee, peering at the little creature.

"I'm your guide to the other side. I warn you that this journey will be no picnic, and it's not kids' play in any way."

Wanting to greet Stitch properly, Will extended his finger, and Stitch placed his hand on it. "Pleased to meet you, Stitch. Do you know where my brother, Sam, is?"

Stitch stepped back. "I don't know, but we need to make

our way to Philidopheos to find out. The question is: are you up to this challenge—this adventure?"

Will turned to each of his friends and swallowed a lump rising in his throat. "If I don't see you again, I want you to know—"

Jules stepped forward and lifted her hand in authority. "Who said you're going alone?" She drew her sword, motioned for the others to do the same, and they all held them high. "And, now, gentlemen, all for one and one for all. That is our motto, is it not?"

Porty glanced at Arrie and shrugged in apparent indifference. Then they both said, "All for one, and one for all."

Will glanced down at Stitch. "Can they come too?"

Stitch lifted his hands and shrugged. "I like group outings, myself. If we are all going, we will need to stand together in front of the wall and say—actually, you don't need to say anything. Just grab each other's hands, and we'll leap through that wall at the same exact time when I say, 'Jump!'"

"What if we don't believe it will work?" Porty blurted, glancing wide-eyed from Stitch to Will.

"If you don't completely let go and trust, you will smack your head against that wall and wish you had," Stitch said with a broad smirk as he climbed back into the pouch, which Will then picked up. "Okay, hold on tight, and one, two, three—jump!"

Four loud thuds against the wall left four thirteen-year-olds on the floor and rubbing their throbbing heads.

Will looked into the pouch.

Staring up at him, Stitch shook his head. "What part of completely letting go and trusting did we not understand?"

Will said, "I think it was me."

"Man, that hurt!" Arrie shouted, jumping to his feet with fire in his eyes. "Is this some kind of a joke?"

"No, Arrie, I think it was my fault," Will said, still rubbing the sore spot on his forehead. "I was a bit skeptical."

A slouching Porty folded his arms across his chest and glanced up sheepishly. "Yeah, it was me too."

Jules picked up her hat and dusted it off. "Let's try again. We can do this. We just have to let go and trust." She got to her feet and peeked inside the pouch. "Can we have one more chance, Stitch? Please?"

Stitch's little elfish hands appeared on the side of the pouch, and his head popped up. He squinted at each one in turn. "Well, I suppose. But this time—"

"We know," Will said. "Trust."

This time, at the word *jump*, Will closed his eyes, grabbed his friends' hands, and, removing all doubt—leaped through the attic wall. Rather than smacking into the wooden slats, Will found himself airborne. Falling! A breeze chilled his face and ruffled his hair. A tingling, sinking sensation made him squeeze his eyes shut. His heart lurched, and he gripped his friends' hands tighter, fearing a crash landing. Was this the end for them?

Chapter 3

A sweet fragrance woke Will. His eyes fluttered open. He and his friends lay on a carpet of green clover dotted with tiny white bell-shaped flowers. He sat up to take in his surroundings.

Jules' hand shot out and latched onto her feathered hat, which lay in the grass beside her. She affixed it to her head and sat upright, strands of long hair in her face. "Phew! What a ride!" Then her eyes opened wide, and her head swiveled from side to side. "What is this place?"

Will gazed out at the magnificently vibrant colors of the endless field. The buzzing from a huge insect tickled his ear. Oh wait . . . it wasn't an insect but a tiny fairy! It tipped one of the bells as it landed and drank dew from the flower. Will continued to stare at the beautiful surroundings, mesmerized by this beautiful sight as Arrie pointed, speechless.

Not surprisingly, Porty awoke last. "Where are we? Will, what are you staring at?"

A muffled sound came from under Will. "Off. Off."

Sitting on the edge of the pouch, Will yanked the strap from his shoulder and shifted off the pouch, and the voice grew louder.

"Finally!" cried the voice.

He opened the pouch.

Stitch stood and peered up at him. "Be careful where you land. Kiggles are breakable, you know."

"Wh-what's a Kiggle?" Will climbed to his feet, making sure not to step on anything.

"I'm a Kiggle," said Stitch as he straightened himself, "and you're not."

Will turned his attention to the little fairy,

dumbfounded, and then pointed to it. "Are fairies real?" he said to Stitch, who clung to the edge of the pouch, peeking his head out.

Porty blinked at Will. "What are you pointing at?"

"Can't you see her?" Will's glance moved from the fairy to his friend. *Why can't Porty see it*?

Stitch shook his head. "Will, only you can see certain things here. When we go through the waters, then your friends will be able to see what they cannot right now."

Jules picked one of the tiny flowers and held it to her nose. "It's so sweet."

Panic flashed on Stitch's face. He scrambled to the top edge of the pouch, leaped onto Jules' arm, and snatched the flower from her.

Jules narrowed her eyes and snapped her words. "Hey, why did you do that?"

Clutching the flower in a fist, Stitch stood back in the clover with his other hand on his hip. "The first lesson here: don't trust anyone." He held up the flower. "This sweet flower smells nice and brings happiness, purity, and humility to those who take in its fragrance, but it's also highly poisonous. The dew from these bells comes from the tears of the Queen for the death of her son, so they also carry the bitterness of her grief and sorrow."

"The Queen?" whispered Jules. "What is this place?"

Grief and sorrow? Will shuddered. Stitch's warning came in stark contrast to their surroundings: the endless meadow, the blue sky, the purple mountains in the distance ... everything so beautiful and in brilliant, unearthly shades. "And why did you say we shouldn't trust anyone?"

Stitch shook his head. "Ah, you trusted me, a Kiggle in a leather pouch hanging in your attic. Not smart."

Before Will could process Stitch's words, he glimpsed movement beside him.

Porty had drawn his sword, which blazed in the sunlight, revealing that it had somehow transformed into a real sword of hard polished steel. Anger flashed in his eyes, and a strange sneer came to his face. He stood over Jules, who still sat in the grass and didn't seem to notice him. Suddenly, the angry-looking Porty raised the sword above Jules as if readying himself to attack her.

Will panicked and drew his own sword. Moving as if by instinct, he plunged it into Porty's side.

Jules drew back and let out an ear-piercing shriek.

A sick feeling stirred in the pit of Will's stomach as he drew the bloody steel from Porty and found bright aqua blood instead of crimson-red blood.

As they stared in horror, a loud thud from behind made them all jump.

Will spun toward the sound, his heart pounding so hard he thought it might burst from his chest.

A plump red-haired boy dressed as a musketeer knelt nearby. He shook his head as he sniffed the flowers in his hand.

Will blinked as if to clear away the mirage. Was his mind playing tricks on him? How could . . . "Porty?" Will struggled to think straight. What was happening to them? Wait! Maybe . . . "Don't smell the flowers!"

Porty froze and released his grip on the flowers, which then fell to the ground. Then he peered at the dead body covered in blue. "What's happening? Where are we?"

The friends breathed a sigh of relief and then surrounded Porty, patting his back to make sure he was real.

"Who . . . What did I just kill?" Will could hardly believe

what he'd done. He'd never killed anything in his entire life, not even a spider. Had he really just killed someone . . . *something*? He hadn't meant to. He'd only wanted to protect Jules.

Porty's eyes opened wide as he studied the figure's face. "You killed *me*?"

Stitch held out his hands. "Calm down, you guys. I told you that we can't trust anyone, right?"

Porty tilted his head as if confused, but the others nodded.

"Will, your instincts were good; you acted quickly to protect Jules. Evil creatures in this land can take on the appearance of someone you trust only to deceive you. That creature may have looked like Porty, but he was a Jacobine. Do you notice anything different about his uniform?"

Arrie rubbed his finger across his lips. "There's no cross on the front, but how would we have known it wasn't Porty?"

Stitch sighed. "You wouldn't."

In the next moment, hair sprouted from the imposter's arms and face, and it started shrinking. The hair grew, replacing even the clothing, and the creature continued shrinking until a little eighteen-inch beast lay before them.

Sure he'd imagined it, Will rubbed his eyes.

Stitch hopped back into the pouch. "We should get started. We have a long journey ahead of us."

Yes, they needed to get on their way. They needed to find his brother. Will adjusted the strap of the pouch on his shoulder and set out, his feet seeming to know which way to go, though his mind questioned everything.

The others followed him, Porty peering over his

shoulder at the dead Jacobine while everyone threw suspicious glances at each other.

Porty came up alongside Will. "You really would have killed me?"

Will shook his head. "Trust me. I would never kill the real you."

Lifting a hand to his mouth, Porty leaned toward Will. "Didn't our friend just tell us not to trust anyone?"

Will whispered, "How do we know he is our friend?"

"I can hear you!" came the muffled voice from the pouch.

Will had no sense of time, at least not in the normal way of gauging it, as they walked and walked through this beautiful but seemingly endless meadow.

"All this walking!" Arrie raced ahead a few steps and blocked Will's way, standing with his hands on his hips. "Are we even heading in the right direction?"

"I wish I knew." Hoping for a sign, Will surveyed their surroundings. A purple mountain range stretched before them, with a single bluish mountain peeking out between the others. "Maybe that's a clue for us."

"After all the blood coming from fake Porty, I've seen enough blue for one day."

After a period of time that felt like hours had passed, they reached the mountain's base. Sheer cliffs rose up from the rocky ground.

"Now what?" Arrie huffed. "Looks like the end of the road for us."

"No, look, we can climb." Jules pointed to a steep, narrow path not too far from them. "That looks like a way up."

"Uh, yeah." Frustration crinkling his brow, Porty flapped his arms at his side. "If you're a billy goat.

Otherwise, this looks way too dangerous."

Will's stomach sank. "I don't think we have a choice." He took the first steps to ascend the steep path.

Chapter 4

With one foot on a tiny ledge and the other wedged in a little crack, Will felt along the face of the blue mountain for something to pull himself up further. Small rocks broke away at his touch and clattered down about twenty feet to where his friends stood watching him from below. His heart raced, and his hands sweated.

Maybe he should go back down and find another way. But no . . . there was no other way. And Sam needed him. When he reached up again, he found a sturdy shelf a foot above him and climbed on.

"We might as well join him," Jules said, and the other two mumbled their agreement.

Scraping sounds and grunts and the occasional stone clattering down the face of the mountain soon followed, but Will refused to glance down. His friends had joined him on this arduous climb.

As Will pulled himself up to a fairly deep shelf, something slithered out of his way. An orange-and-blue lizard-like creature stared at him and then disappeared between cracks. He sucked in a breath, startled.

A little further up, as he reached for a sturdy root, something living in the root mass swiped at his hands. Will drew his hand back just as the creature—some black-and-red thing with razor-like fur—peeked out from between roots. Tired and frustrated, Will hissed at the creature, which then scattered off.

"What are you hissing at, Will?" Jules shouted up to him.

He pulled himself to the next ledge. "Oh, just some wild animal trying to kill us."

In unison, the other three started making loud hissing sounds, warily peering around for signs of danger.

At long last, Will pulled himself up to the top of the mountain, a narrow plateau with a lone tree and a breathtaking view all around. He reached down to offer each of his friends a hand. Finally, the four stood to take in the grandeur of the scene. They now stood among the clouds, able to see in every direction. An emerald-green river wound its way through the lush, pristine valley below.

Arrie, who stood closer to the far edge, cleared his throat. "Uh, Will . . ." He peered down the opposite side of the mountain. "This doesn't look right. It's way too steep to climb down. We'll never reach the river this way."

Will came to his side, and his stomach leaped. The cliff went straight down to the valley far below. "Yeah, we can't go down that way." Will turned in a circle, searching for another way down, but found nothing. "Hey, Stitch . . ." He yanked open the pouch and looked inside to talk to his new little friend, but Stitch was gone. "Hey, where'd he go?"

Will fished inside the pouch for the pewter cup. Should he use another one of the wishes? As he wrapped his fingers around the goblet, he brushed something else. "I didn't think this pouch held anything besides the goblet and Stitch." He pulled the new item out, discovering a leather-bound book. "What's this?"

Arrie squatted by the edge, watching a rust-colored stone he had dropped take its long flight down. "Can Stitch please give us a clue for how to get down from here? That's a dangerous drop, and it'll start getting cold up here soon."

"He's not here." Will inspected the leather book's front and back, embossed with designs of strange creatures.

"What? Isn't he supposed to be our guide? We don't

even know where we're going." Arrie backed away from the edge and flung his hands in the air.

"What's that?" Standing at Will's shoulder, Jules pulled the book from his grasp and opened it to the first page of blank yellowed parchment paper. "I don't know how this will help us."

"Trust," Will murmured to himself.

"Trust who?" stammered Porty, running his hand through his hair. "Stitch said we shouldn't trust anyone, at least not right away. Maybe we shouldn't have trusted him? Maybe he wanted us to die up here?"

Jules approached Will. "Why did you say 'trust'? What are you thinking, Will?"

Will rubbed his forehead, scrambling to think of what to do next. "Stitch said not to trust anyone, but Poppie said I needed to let go and trust. Maybe I need to trust this pouch—or maybe this book?" Will took the book back, opened it up again, and stared at the blank page. Suddenly, words appeared! Unfortunately, he couldn't decipher the ancient-looking writing.

Not giving up, he closed his eyes and tried to picture the page, trusting that it would provide a clue or lead them safely down the other side of the mountain. Just as he opened his eyes, an odd-looking vulture-like bird with black feathers and a bright-red head swooped down and sent a splat of goo into Will's eyes.

"Ugh!" Panic set in as he furiously wiped the sticky green goo from his eyes. "Trust, trust, trust," he said to calm himself. Wiping the last bit of goo, he opened his eyes. The ancient characters on the page were now brightly colored, and he could understand them. Will read the first line aloud. *Apart from me, you can do nothing, but I will always be with you.*

"Who is 'me'? How does that help us?" Arrie's shoulders drooped.

Porty gazed down the face of the cliff, which easily measured several thousand feet, and shook his head. "This is impossible. We have to go back, guys."

Will shut out their words and continued to focus on the page. Suddenly, a green vine appeared below the writing, winding its way down and then off the page to the ground. The vine grew longer and longer before their eyes, making its way over the edge of the cliff. Its thickness and branches made it sturdy and gave them something to hold onto, but it only reached about ten feet down the side of the cliff.

Arrie rolled his eyes. "And how does that help?"

Will closed the book, stuffed it into the pouch, grabbed onto the vine that clung to the side of the mountain, and began climbing down.

"What's he doing?" groaned Arrie.

In a shaky voice, Jules said, "Hold on, Will. I'm right behind you," as she grabbed a vine branch and placed her foot securely on the next one.

Arrie and Porty glanced at each other, shrugged, and followed her lead.

With every step Will took, the vine grew a little bit longer, making its way further down the side of the cliff.

Porty and Arrie crept down the steep rock face, holding tightly to the vine.

"How do we know we can trust this vine to hold? There's so little for it to grab onto. What if it doesn't hold or doesn't keep growing?" Arrie shouted down.

"I'm not so sure about this," Porty bellowed. "The branches are starting to pull away from the cliff wall!"

Before Porty completed his sentence, the vine at his

level had released from the wall. Both he and Arrie, clinging to the vine, swung away from the ragged cliff wall, screaming.

Will's heart leaped. If they fell, it would mean certain death. Despite the intensity of the panic, the branches he and Jules held onto remained firmly fixed. "Arrie! Porty! Stop yelling. Do what I say. Hold on and take a deep breath. Close your eyes, and trust that the vine will hold—it will not let us down. Just try it!"

"O-o-okay!" yelled Arrie, letting out a deep breath as he gripped the vine.

"I-I think it might be working!" Porty called out. "The branches are moving back toward the cliff and grabbing on."

Will heard deep sighs from above as the immediate crisis ended, and they all resumed their long climb down. Will's trust that the vine would hold continued to increase, while red- and peach-colored berries and other unusual fruit started to grow from the branches.

They hadn't eaten since sitting down in the attic room with their candy piles, however long ago that was. Will's stomach made a loud growl.

"Look at all this fruit growing on the vine." Clinging one-handed to the vine, Porty snatched a round, purplish fruit with his other hand. "Do you think it's safe to eat?"

"I don't know," Jules said. "I guess one of us could find out."

"I'll do it." Porty took the first bite. "It's delicious," he shouted down to them.

Everyone laughed.

Will popped a small peach-colored fruit into his mouth, and an explosion of flavor burst on his tongue. He shoved a few fruits into his pouch and peered down at the long descent ahead. They had to keep going.

Once he finally reached the ground, he stepped out of the way as the others climbed down. The sky had turned a deeper shade of blue, and the air had chilled, making him shiver.

Will checked out the area of green bushes and scattered trees in the dwindling light. "I think we're going to have to camp here."

Arrie tossed the pit aside. "Porty and I can get some wood to build a fire before this place gets any colder."

"Or spookier," added Porty, scanning his surroundings through round eyes.

And dark it got as Arrie and Porty stumbled back to Will and Jules with their arms full of branches. They couldn't even see one another in the pitch-black of the valley.

"What good is this wood without matches?" Will reached into the pouch to feel around. He'd found the book and metal cup. Maybe he'd find something else. "I wish we had a spark."

Suddenly, tiny dots of light appeared like fireflies encircling them.

"Wow, I've never seen a creature this small." The points of light reflected in Jules' wide-open eyes.

Several creatures landed on the pile of kindling . . . and a flame caught hold! What may have been the leader of these tiny creatures hovered in front of them and bowed, wings fluttering.

"Thank you." Will smiled as they flew away into the night. Welcoming the warmth, he sat by the campfire, and the others joined him. The small flames became a roaring fire that lit up a circle for a cozy gathering.

Arrie laughed. "You're like Mister Magic Man. Snap your fingers, and fire appears!"

Everyone laughed except for Will, who reached into the pouch to retrieve the old pewter cup to hold it to the light.

"What's wrong?" Arrie stopped laughing.

Will's shoulders slumped, and he lowered the cup to his lap. There for everyone to see was the finely scrolled number on the face of the cup that now read *8*.

Jules held her palms to the fire. "You'll have to be careful about using those wishes, but this sure feels better than freezing to death out here."

Nodding, Will pulled from the pouch some of the fruit he had picked off the vine on the way down the mountain face. He shared it as the golden flames illuminated the faces of his best friends. At times, his friends could irritate him, and he wished he could change some things about each one, but, at this moment, he was grateful to have them by his side.

"Will, where are we going next?" Porty bit into a peach-like fruit.

Will tossed a twig into the fire and slouched. "I have no idea. I always feel better when I can plan out what I'm going to do, but I have absolutely no clue about this. I should've never asked you to come. Sam's my brother, and it's my fault he's gone, and this whole thing seems way too dangerous."

Jules watched Will intently as he spoke.

Arrie tapped Porty's arm and pointed to Jules.

"Remember—you didn't ask us," said Jules. "You just have friends stupid enough to follow you to the ends of the earth."

Still wishing he hadn't allowed his friends to come on this dangerous adventure, Will gave her a sad little smile. "It certainly feels like that's where we're going . . . to the ends of the earth. Whatever happens, I want you guys to know how much I appreciate it. Really." He gazed directly into each pair of eyes to communicate how much he meant it. To break the awkward seriousness of the moment, he stopped at Porty. "You are Porty—right?"

Porty glanced around uncomfortably. "Yeah! And I don't have blue goop coming out of me either—but how do I know you guys are you guys? Well, you know what I mean."

"He's got a point," said Arrie.

"Well, there's one way to tell," Jules said. "Each of us can share something secret about ourselves that only one other person here knows."

A secret popped into Will's mind, but did he really want to share it? It wasn't a secret without reason.

Jules broke the silence. "I guess I should start since it was my idea. Well, here goes. I overheard my parents arguing about having another child when I was seven. My mother wanted a baby badly, and my father snapped, 'I don't want another girl. I don't know what to do with her, and I don't think you are built for making boys.' I was devastated. He'd always seemed distant and rarely paid attention to me, but it was . . ." Jules hesitated, her voice changing as if there were a sudden, painful lump in her throat. ". . . something I really craved from him. That was the day I stood in front of the mirror, cut off all my hair, and tried out for the boy's baseball team. I just wanted him to be proud of me." A tear ran down her cheek.

Will remembered the day she'd tried out for the baseball team. It was the day he'd first met her.

Porty shifted his position and hunched over. "I didn't think we were going that deep. I was just going to talk about the time I tried on my mom's bra when I was nine to see how it worked, and Arrie walked in."

Jules started laughing and couldn't stop.

Arrie raised his eyebrows. "I think he looked good in it!"

Will burst out laughing so hard that tears streamed down his face.

Arrie and Porty joined the laughter and began to howl. Porty never had a problem making people laugh, even at his own expense.

As the night drew on, Will's eyelids grew heavy, and he lay down on the ground, looking up at the stars. There were more stars in the evening sky than he could ever remember seeing.

"I don't see the dippers." Porty folded his arms behind his head, gazing up at the sky.

"Huh. The stars do seem brighter, though. I don't know if that's the moon or not"—Arrie pointed— "but it almost looks like the shape of a woman standing on it."

Porty laughed. "Everything seems like the shape of a woman to you these days."

Jules giggled. "You didn't tell us your secret, Arrs."

Arrie exhaled and continued gazing at the sky as if pondering the vastness of the universe above and around him. "I was hoping you'd forget. What if I have no secrets?"

They all threw twigs or pebbles at him.

Jules said, "Everyone has secrets—probably too many of them. Fess up, bucko-boy."

"All right. I had a brother who was eight years older than me. He didn't have much time for me, which I get now, but I really looked up to him. He was the coolest person I knew, and I loved wearing any old hand-me-downs from him. I wanted to be just like him. Well, he hung around with friends who weren't really *friends,* if you know what I mean. I don't know—I think he got lost and had more fights with my folks because of it. His moods would go way up and way down. I didn't really understand it—I still don't." Arrie stopped. A comet shot across the sky, leaving a bright trail behind it. Then he composed himself. "One night, before he got his driver's license, he took my folks' car out, and I guess he was driving it fast, really fast. Too fast."

Will glanced up. "I didn't know you had an older brother. I'm sorry."

"No one in this town does. My parents didn't know if it was an accident or a suicide, but we left and moved here. No one talks about him. Jules knows because I let it slip out one day. At least I know I can trust her."

Jules faced Arrie and smiled, touching his shoulder with an outstretched hand.

A sudden flash of light in the distance broke the moment. It came again, like a blast of fire across the wide river.

"Holy smokes," stammered Porty, pushing himself up. "What was that?"

"I don't know, but it wasn't just smoke," replied Will. "That's for sure."

Will watched for a moment more, but the flash didn't come again. The warmth of their campfire and the surrounding darkness soon eased his fear. He rested his head on the ground, finding it surprisingly soft. Both physical and emotional exhaustion overtook him, and he drifted off to the sound of the others snoring.

Chapter 5

Will woke first to the morning light and struggled to move his body. Something held his arms and legs in place. He lifted his head to try to identify it—yuck! A spongy, web-like blanket covered him from his neck to his feet. Panic giving speed to his actions, he peeled the sticky web off his body and jumped to his feet. The cool air brought goosebumps to his arms, so he shuffled closer to the remaining embers of their campfire. Guess it was warmer under that strange blanket. But how—?

"Hey, what's this?" Arrie said, punching at the blanket wrapped around him.

"It's so soft and warm." Jules sat up, looking like a butterfly peeking out of its cocoon.

"Ugh. No." Porty twisted and flopped on the ground, struggling to free himself. "Help, someone."

Laughing, Will came over and grabbed the edge of the blanket nearest his neck. "You've just got to peel it off like this." Within seconds, he freed Porty.

As Will turned, he glimpsed something he hadn't noticed before. The entrance to an overgrown path stood before him, twisting its way to a river, which appeared more like an emerald-green lake from there. Will pulled his pouch strap over his shoulder and checked inside to see if Stitch might have returned. Nope. No sign of the little Kiggle. He slid his steel sword into its holster on his hip.

"How do we know where to go next?" Porty spun himself around.

Will didn't know. He retrieved the leather-bound book from the pouch and opened it, surprised to find the second page now filled with writing and pictures. He held the old parchment page out to show it to the rest.

"It's blank." Arrie furrowed his brow.

"Oh, yeah. All right, let me see if this gives us any clues." Then he read, *The lighted path beneath your feet will lead you to the shore and a wild-looking man whom you can trust to point the way to the kingdom.*

As he finished reading, a soft glow caught his attention. Swirling points of light illuminated the nearby overgrown path.

"Oh, look!" Jules, sounding awestruck, strolled to the path and reached toward one and then another little firefly-like ball. "These little fairies helped us start our fire last night."

"Their path leads to that green lake." Porty flung an arm out, pointing.

"Guess we should follow it, huh?" Arrie peered down the path.

"Shouldn't we have breakfast first?" Porty rubbed his belly.

Arrie shook his head and led the way, taking the path with long, casual strides. As they neared the river, he stopped until Will came to his side. "Uh, maybe not."

Ahead on the riverbank, a two-legged beast with a tall staff stood gesturing wildly, talking to himself like a madman.

"I don't think that's our guy," murmured Arrie.

The tiny fairies stretched out their wee arms, each pointing toward the wild beast.

"I think maybe he is our guy." Will took a deep breath, mustering courage, and proceeded down the path, the rest following apprehensively.

"I don't know about this," whispered Arrie.

As they got closer, the creature—a man in animal skins,

covered in mud—turned and jumped at the sight of Will.

Will jumped back.

The man then aimed his staff, which looked more like a hunting spear, at Will and grunted. "You're the one I've been waiting for."

Will's shoulders tightened, a spooked feeling overcoming him until the man made eye contact. Then his shoulders relaxed, and he regained his peace. The man seemed like someone who knew him well. Will nodded. "We are looking for my brother. Do you know where we are to go?"

"Yes. It's a place I cannot go. You must reach the river's other side to enter the kingdom's path."

Will nodded. "We saw flashes of light last night. Do you know anything about them?"

The wild man narrowed his eyes.

Confused, Will scanned the area and spotted a small boat on the shore. "Do we get across by boat?" He pointed to it.

The man shook his head and used his staff to direct their attention across the river to a giant creature, too difficult to make out at that distance. Suddenly, a ball of fire roared from the creature's mouth and shot across the river's width.

Frightened, Will jumped back and fell to the ground as the flames nearly reached him.

"Many have tried to cross by boat, but none have made it before being turned to ashes by the beast, Chimera. You'll need to pass far below the surface, immersed in a watery grave of darkness. You will be frightened, but you must trust the light to give you the strength and the seal for your mission."

Will glanced to his friends for help. "What seal? Do you

know what our mission is?"

The man nodded but said nothing.

"To find Sam?" Will wanted him to explain. "This way will lead us to Sam, right?"

"There is much more."

Jules squinted, fixing her stare on the fire-breathing monster across the way. "Sir, I don't mean to be a scaredy-cat, but even if we can get across this river underwater without drowning, that beast will be waiting for us on the other shore. Won't we be in more danger?"

The man nodded. The flames came closer, fanning out as they crossed the river. The fire-breathing beast was now clearly focused on them. "Yes, you will be in much danger." He held his spear out to Arrie. "You have been in the games?"

Arrie rubbed his chin. "Games? I toss the javelin for the track team, but—"

He handed Arrie the spear. "At the end of this spear is a lead point. You will have only one chance to launch this into Chimera's mouth as he readies to burn you with flames. The lead will melt as it enters the heat."

Porty shuddered and threw Will a wide-eyed look.

Will shrugged but tried to convey hope. Arrie had never won a javelin throwing meet, and everyone knew it.

"Before you plunge into these waters," the man said, "leave me with one thing."

"What is that?" Will trembled inside. How could they possibly cross the river alive? What would they have to do next?

"Each of you must whisper to me –and only me – your biggest regret in life, and you will be unburdened by it during your crossing. No one will ever know what you tell me, and it must be your biggest regret."

Jules leaned toward the stranger first to share her most confidential regret. Afterward, the man put his hand on her forehead. Porty went next, and then Arrie.

Finally, Will slowly approached the man, his chest tightening with anxiety and shame as he whispered his regret.

The man stood back and looked directly into his eyes. "It must be your worst."

Will jerked back. *How could he know I had a deeper regret than that?* Resigning himself, he closed his eyes, took a deep breath, and then leaned in to whisper his deepest regret. The wild-looking man marked his forehead as a tear ran down Will's cheek. Then the man stepped back and faded away like a foggy vapor of dust until he completely disappeared.

Porty shook his head. "Well, that was strange. Now we have to cross this." Porty flung a hand in the direction of the river. "And I can't even swim. Even if I could, that's a long way to go underwater. It must be a mile wide. A watery grave, the man said. That's exactly what this is gonna be."

Will stood frozen, staring at the spot where the man had turned to dust before his very eyes. "I don't think he would lead us to this if there were another way."

Arrie clutched the spear and practiced his throw. "Whatever happened to not trusting anyone?"

Will and his companions slogged into the warm water until it reached their shoulders. Then, they each took a deep breath, submerged themselves, and began to swim. Light and heat from the Chimera's flames penetrated the upper layers, the scalding heat forcing them deeper into the darker and cooler waters, guided only by the small flickers of light that only Will could see ahead of them.

Soon, Will's eyes grew accustomed to what felt like a dark cavernous liquid tomb. Strange-looking fluorescent pink fish with huge eyes and fins swam by. Spiky yellow creatures clung to feathery plants Will didn't recognize. They passed the charred remains of a ship sunk half in the riverbed. It had likely tried to cross the river until it met with Chimera's flames. As they continued, it struck Will how they could hold their breaths this long, never mind that Porty could now swim.

They continued downward and reached the bottom of the waters, where darkness surrounded them. The next moment, several pairs of green glowing eyes appeared and surrounded them. Will fought to overcome panic as he tried to assess the situation. The creatures moved closer, their glowing eyes making their scaly lizard bodies and horned heads visible in the murky green water. Their frog-like arms and legs swirled and kicked with pointy webbed fingers and toes as they swam around the friends.

Will tried to continue on, but the creatures tightened their circle around them. They weren't here to provide a hospitable escort. They wanted to stop them. Wanting to drive the creatures back, Will drew his sword and thrust it toward the ones blocking his way.

In response, the creatures zipped toward Arrie and lashed at him with their long legs and arms. The spear fell from Arrie's hand and drifted toward the bottom. Arrie tried grabbing it, his arms moving slowly through the water. The creatures' long double-pointed red-and-green lizard-like tongues shot out and pierced his neck and body. Arrie stopped moving, his arms and legs hanging limply around his facedown body drifting near the bottom of the river.

Determined to protect his friend, Will attacked with his sword. Jules and Porty followed suit until each creature was dead.

Dread filled Will as he turned his attention to Arrie. He grabbed him by the arm and shook him, but Arrie did not respond. A sharp pain pierced Will's heart. Arrie was dead.

Panic now filled his friends' eyes as the danger of their journey abruptly felt more real than ever. Arrie lay lifeless, and Jules' face scrunched up with sadness, the water stealing her tears. Porty dragged Arrie's body into his arms, staring at Will as if for some sign of hope.

Will felt helpless to do anything, but time was short. Without hesitation, he reached into the pouch and wrapped his fingers around the handle of the pewter cup. He quickly wished that Arrie would not be dead, but nothing happened.

Grief clouding his thoughts and unsure what to do, Will decided to keep swimming. Maybe they'd all die before they reached the other side, but what else could they do?

Tugging Arrie's body along with him, Porty followed. Jules came along last, carrying the spear. Will led the way through a dark tunnel-like cave that angled upward, the water getting warmer. They emerged from the cave in shallow water and soon found themselves able to stand on the rocky riverbed. Just before they broke the water's surface, Will grabbed the spear from Jules, wanting to prepare himself for Chimera.

Then the three of them waded from the river together, Will gripping the spear, and Porty and Jules carried Arrie as they cried.

With its great dragon-like body, the terrifying Chimera stood a mere twenty yards away. As the black eyes in its lion-like head turned toward the four invaders of his domain, it let out a ferocious screech, flapped its large bat-like wings, and thrashed its spiky tail.

Will's heart beat faster, gripping the spear tighter as fear and anger filled him. He sloshed through the shallow water to more solid ground. His friends hurried toward a boulder just above the riverbank.

Chimera screeched again, hot flames shooting from its nostrils and scorching the earth in a trail heading for them.

Will dove out of the way and rolled back onto his feet, narrowly escaping the fire. The creature turned its attention to the others as Will regained his footing and readied the spear for battle. He reared back with the spear, but then something tugged at it from behind.

"I've got this."

It was Arrie, somehow alive. He took the spear from Will and raced toward the beast, holding it like a javelin.

Chimera turned and fixed its gaze on Arrie with laser-like focus. As it opened its mouth, revealing spiky teeth, about to let out a fiery blast, Arrie took two giant lunging steps forward and tossed the spear with all his might, letting out a loud, "Ahhhhh!"

Flames shot from Chimera's mouth just as the spear reached its target. The iron tip melted from the intensity of the heat, opening a hole in the beast's throat, sending it to the ground, twisting and writhing with ear-piercing screams. Then its long neck and lion-like head flopped to the ground, and it fell silent.

A great sigh of relief escaped Will at the sight of the conquered beast, but even greater joy filled his heart. Arrie was alive. How had they survived the long swim into the depths of this river, and how had they conquered this beast? Arrie seemed stronger, freer, and more confident than before entering the waters, and Porty had made the underwater swim with Arrie in his arms despite his inability to swim. Still catching their breath, the four comrades came together in a collective embrace. As they separated, a white bird hovered over Will and seemed to stare right at him for several seconds before flying off.

"I wonder what that was about?" Arrie watched it fly away.

Jules glanced down and smiled. "I can see the tiny fairies now! And the colors seem brighter—and, somehow, I feel stronger. Where do we go from here?"

Will took a deep breath, reached into his pouch, and drew out the leather-bound book, perplexed to find it dry. He opened it to the third page.

Before Will could read it, Jules exclaimed, "Hey, I can see the writing now!"

Arrie and Porty said they could see it but couldn't decipher the words.

Will laughed. "At least you still need me for something." As Will stared at the page, the writing became clear.

A kingdom has been lost and scattered. It now awaits a new king who must prove himself worthy and faithful in a place where nothing grows.

Jules tilted her head. "What do you think that means?"

Will shrugged. "We never seem to know until it happens. I'm not sure which way to go except forward."

As they trekked forward, Porty draped his arm around Arrie. "I'm glad to see you alive after you died."

"What? I died?"

"And you're heavier than I thought," quipped Porty with raised eyebrows.

Chapter 6

As the distance from the river grew, the trees thinned out, thorny bushes replacing them. Then rocks replaced the bushes. No rabbits, squirrels, or even strange red-and-black furry creatures scurried about the empty wilderness. Their path wound through a barren area where dozens of perfectly round rocks were scattered.

Porty stood on one stone, playfully balancing himself like a posed statue. Then he suddenly jumped off, eyes open wide with a look of fright. "That rock moved!"

Arrie laughed. "You're imagining things, Porty."

Porty's eyes practically bulged from their sockets. "No, I felt it!"

As they stared at the rock, it rolled on its own and unfolded into a grotesque, stocky creature, less than half the size of a human. "Watch what you stand on, big man," the creature said in a strange language they could somehow understand.

Porty ducked his head. "I'm really sorry, but you did look like a rock."

"That's because we're hiding." The creature's skin was coarse, its eyes wide and black, but it did not scare Will.

"We?" asked Jules.

Before the creature answered, dozens of other round-shaped rocks turned and unfolded into creatures like it.

Will moved closer to Jules and the others, a bit uncomfortable surrounded by these small, wide-eyed rock people.

"Yes, we—as you can see. We are the Lydians. We were once part of a great kingdom that lost its way, and now we are scattered through the lands and hunted. That is why we hide." With eyes widened, the other Lydian creatures nodded in agreement.

Will's brow tightened. "Kingdom? Where is this kingdom?"

The short, stocky creature stepped forward, and Will spotted a sad earnestness in his eyes under his bushy brows. "It is destroyed. Our great people's once lush and bountiful land is now a barren desert and wilderness. No life exists except for the evil one who seeks to destroy the remaining scattered members and any hope of a new king."

"Why do you think a new king is coming?" Jules leaned down with her hands on her knees.

The creature glanced at his tribe and responded, "There is one more powerful than who lives there now. It is said that he made a promise to the ancestors of the kingdom's scattered peoples."

Will scratched his head. "Who is this more powerful person?"

"He has no name that can capture him, but we call him the Giver, and the evil one the Taker. The kingdom and its people were once happy, living in peace, but they drifted away from the Giver, thinking they no longer needed him and stopped trusting him. The Taker promised them a better life if they followed him instead and told lies to undermine their trust in the Giver. People became more suspicious and selfish and broke into groups that fought with each other. They put themselves above the kingdom that had been a family. As this trusted bond broke, things began to decay. Crops wouldn't grow, and small groups left for the false promise of something better."

Jules peered around at all the creatures. "Are the Lydians one of those groups?"

The creature nodded. "We've been wandering, hiding, and living in fear for a very long time—waiting for the chosen one to defeat the Taker and restore unity in the kingdom."

Will drifted in thought, wondering if the Giver was someone he could trust in this strange world or if the name was a trick. His attention snapped back as the creature warned them.

"If you value your life, I wouldn't recommend proceeding any further. The Taker is a formidable force and exceedingly deceptive. You won't know what is real and true if you encounter him. Only unburdened people can possibly pass, but no creature with fault can do so. His helpers will attack, appearing at the last second when it's too late to defend yourself. They can appear as pale-green horned Grindylows in water."

Will raised his hand and interrupted. "If they have lizard skin and frog-like webbed hands and feet, I think we've met them."

"That would be them. You are very fortunate to have survived. Watch out also for Stymph birds with razor-sharp feathers in the air and the Fear Dearies, all red from head to toe when visible. They can also appear like someone you trust. And they have many weapons at their disposal, making them most dangerous."

"If you are trying to scare us, you're doing a great job. My name is Will." He turned to his friends, pointing at each in turn. "This is Jules, Porty, and Arrie. What's your name?"

"We don't have names these days, but I call myself 'Beno.' Can I ask where you are going?"

"I'm searching for my brother, Sam. I don't know where he is, but we need to cross to the other side of this land. Is there another way to go?"

Beno shook his head. "This is the only way, but no one has survived it. Your brother could not have gone this way unless..."

Will glanced down. The lights from the tiny fairies shone in the direction of the deserted wilderness. "I can't give up hope. We have to try."

"Yeah, we've got to try," Arrie said. Jules and Porty also gave their assent.

"We wish you well," one of the Lydians said, the others nodding.

Beno escorted them to the edge of the land. "You will be tested greatly. Be on guard at all times!"

Will nodded and made a move to turn toward the wilderness.

Beno stopped him, grabbing Will's trouser leg with a stubby hand. "The struggles will be as dangerous internally as they are externally." His bushy brows lowered over eyes filled with sincerity and concern.

Will thought about Beno's warning that *only unburdened people could possibly pass* and the regret he had shared with the wild man in animal skins at the river. Were they able to make that crossing because he had confessed his regret to the man? He didn't know, but sharing his guilt about wishing his brother would disappear didn't remove the feeling or his responsibility.

The four friends proceeded into a wilderness of death and destruction. Faded signs of a once vibrant life littered the sandy landscape. Will strode between a tumbleweed and a skeleton of some animal, trying to avoid kicking up sand with every step. Soon, the Lydians disappeared from view, and sand stretched out in every direction.

Jules tugged her hat lower, the wide brim shielding her eyes from the sun's scorching heat. Arrie wiped his forehead with his arm, and Porty moaned as he dragged one foot and then the other through the sand.

As the sun sank into the empty horizon, the air chilled. Will shivered and buttoned up his musketeer jacket. Feeling compelled to keep going rather than stop for the night, they marched onward, not even knowing if they were heading in the right direction.

For several days, the scorching sun's heat seemed endless. It wore them down during the day, while the frosty evening air made them shiver without shelter at night. With no food, water, or sleep, the journey began to take its toll on each of them.

To avoid feeling hopeless, Will continued checking the book in his pouch, but no help was forthcoming.

Porty dropped to the ground. "I can't do this. We need one of those wishes now."

Jules and Arrie nodded.

Will reached into the pouch to grab the goblet, but his hand could only feel the book's leather cover. He pulled it out, flipped it open, and glanced at the next page. This time, handwritten words were on it.

Do not lose your trust; I will always be with you.

Will sank to the warm sand at his feet. "What does that mean? We're here alone with nothing in sight except sand and sun. The fairies aren't even with us to let us know if we're heading the right way."

Stooping by Will's side, Jules rested her hand on his shoulder. "We're not alone. We have each other and haven't been let down along the way yet."

Will pulled himself back up. "You're right. I have a feeling we're going to need all the wishes we have left, and that writing in the notebook showed up for a reason. Trust. We have to trust. This isn't easy, but we must find Sam."

Porty sat up from where he'd fallen in the sand and shook his head. "I'm done. I'm hot. I'm cold. I'm hungry and tired, and the book says to trust. Who are we supposed to trust? I can't see doing this anymore when we can snap our fingers and have some food—and maybe get back home."

In the next moment, the airflow changed as if someone or something moved around them. Will, now on high alert, glanced every which way. Something surrounded them, an eerie specter, but it didn't show itself.

A haunting voice hissed, "I commend your s-s-s-strength and persis-s-s-stence. It should be rewarded, don't you think?"

Will spun toward the voice. "Who are you?'

"I am here to help you. No one else cares-s-s-s-s about you."

Will shifted his eyes, trying to follow the voice, but saw nothing but air and sand.

"Who are you talking to?" Jules threw wide-eyed glances all around.

"I can't see it, but I sense its presence." Arrie also looked around. "Will, what is it?"

After turning in a full circle, obviously not seeing it either, Porty shuffled closer to the group.

"What's going on?" asked Arrie.

Will squinted and focused on the voice. "Are you here to show us the way?"

"Better than that, *ssssss,* I can help you do it yours-s-self, help you get food for the journey and find your brother. Use one of your wishes to turn this s-s-s-sand into the most delicious food you've ever tasted. You can do *anything* on your own. You don't need anyone. Just give me the book; you won't need it any longer."

"How do you know about Sam? Are you saying I can't trust this book?"

"Noooo," hissed the specter. "But you can trus-s-s-s-st me. Think of how good that food would taste after all these days without any. Think of your friends-s-s-s-s, how hungry they are."

Will's senses filled with a strong temptation to trust the voice and use a wish. He would still have plenty left. It seemed like the right thing to do until the words of Stitch came to mind, and then the message in the book. *Trust.* He clutched the pouch tight. "There are more important things in life than the food we eat. I don't trust you. I think you're trying to deceive us."

"You are fools-s-s-s!" bellowed the voice.

With a final hiss, the presence disappeared.

Porty glanced up at Will, shielding his eyes from the sun. "Who were you talking to? Are we getting food?"

Will shook his head. "This way, guys. We can do this." He led the way through the barrenness and unrelenting desert heat until another night fell, still without food or water. They finally had to stop and try to get some sleep, despite the chill in the air and the hungry ache of their empty bellies.

Morning arrived, and Will woke to cool temperatures and slivers of sunshine, not the heat of the past few mornings that had him feeling like a pancake on a griddle. Sitting up, he blinked a few times, not trusting his eyes. Tall, majestic trees surrounded them. They'd spent the night in a heavily wooded forest carpeted by cool green moss and red berries. He hopped to his feet and tapped each of his mates to wake them. "Hey, guys, you'll never believe this."

"How did we get here?" Arrie's mouth hung open in awe.

Jules got up, jumped on the spongy carpet of moss, and smiled. "This is amazing. And look at how tall these trees are!" She stretched and twisted her body, peering upward. "I can't even see the tops."

Arrie turned himself in a complete circle. "So, what do we do? How can we tell which direction to head in?"

Will pulled out the book, hoping for guidance, and opened to the next page. Yes! A new message!

In your darkest moment, do not doubt. I will always be with you. Even when you think I have abandoned you.

Not sure what to make of the message, Will closed the book and stuffed it back into the pouch. He turned, peering through the dense forest in every direction until he saw the brightest sunbeam breaking through. "Let's go that way."

Arrie, Porty, and Jules exchanged glances, and each shrugged, no better ideas forthcoming, so they followed Will. Jules continued to gaze upward as if marveling at the sheer height of the trees. The deeper they walked, the darker the woods became until it seemed like a moonless night, despite being early in the day.

As they struggled to follow the path, red dots of light appeared in the dark canopy above. More red dots joined the first few, becoming a swarm above them. Maybe they would lead the way. The swarm of red lights dropped lower in the sky, growing bigger as they approached. The lights—no, not lights, eyes of fire!—belonged to giant birds with feathers that glinted like sharp metal razors. One bird swooped directly toward Will!

Will ducked out of the way and shouted, "The Stymph birds Beno warned us about! Take cover! Watch out for their feathers!" Four razor feathers pierced the thick tree trunk next to Will as the friends scrambled to find hiding places. He hit the ground and crawled behind the tree, but several more birds bore down on them from between the trees, causing adrenaline to flood Will's chest.

"Ouch!" screeched Jules as a razor-edged feather sliced through the air. She grabbed her arm, where a streak of blood seeped through her sleeve. "That burns!" She shot up in anger and swung her sword at a Stymph swooping down for another attack. Her sword clipped its wings, and the Stymph's face contorted in pain as it retreated awkwardly, flapping only one wing.

As another swooped in, with the smell of Jules' blood, Will leaped to his feet to fight off the attack.

Arrie and Porty finally shook themselves from their frozen stupors, glanced at each other, and joined the fight. The attacks intensified, and so did the number of hits from the dangerous and not-so-feathery wings.

"There are too many of them!" Porty shouted.

"And we've got one sword each while they have a gazillion razor-sharp feathers!" Arrie shouted.

The four huddled together. Will hunched over Jules to protect her, his heart beating rapidly, feeling as if this was it.

But in the next moment, the attacks stopped. The flying creatures drew back. Rather than obtain certain victory, they surrounded the four from a distance, glaring at them through fiery eyes.

A hissing sound and foreboding filled the air.

Will glanced around, not sure where the voice came from.

"S-s-s-seems like your trusted one has abandoned you. You are s-s-s-seconds away from a very painful and bloody death. If you trust him to protect you, then let him prove it."

Will glanced toward his friends but didn't respond.

The specter hissed, "You are a s-s-s-smart boy. You wouldn't want your friends to die. Isn't that what friends do—protect each other? I can s-s-s-see some doubt in you."

At the word *doubt*, Will remembered the last thing he had read in the book. He turned toward the specter, holding his sword in front of him. "Do what you will, but I will never doubt, and I will never fall for your deceit and tricks," he yelled, slicing his sword through the air. As he stood tall, the large, ferocious birds returned to finish off their four victims in the most painful way possible.

Jules, Arrie, and Porty jumped up to join Will, standing back-to-back with swords drawn.

Jules held out her sword and shouted, "If we have to go, then all for one, and—"

Before the boys could finish the line, the birds swooped in. Almost to their mark, a new ally joined forces with the friends. The trees swung into action, their branches swinging like the arms of giants, striking down one bird and then another. Red points of light scattered as other birds flew away, retreating until none remained.

Will stood stunned. What would happen next? Would these giant trees now attack them and end their journey in this dark wilderness? The others clung together for protection while he was the first to stare directly at one of the imposing trees. Surprisingly, he could make out the image of a face in the bark.

The mouth on the face moved, and crinkles formed by

the eyes. "Do not worry," the tree said, "you are safe with us, but they will not give up." The tree pointed to the trail with one of its branches. "Take a safe passage on the route the fairies light, and we will protect you."

Still shaken, they turned to head in that direction, but Will stopped and turned back. "Thank you."

All the trees around them bowed like humble servants helping fellow creatures on their journey. Jules smiled and waved as she touched the outstretched branch, then she and Will caught up with Arrie and Porty.

Chapter 7

The towering trees provided safe passage through the woods. Some handed the tired and hungry travelers fruit from their branches for their journey. At night, as the temperature dropped, other trees sacrificed their older branches to make a campfire, which the tiny fairies started with their sparks.

Now and then, red eyes appeared among the foliage in the distance, but Will didn't let it bother him. The trees provided safety. They could all relax. He sat and gazed at the warm glow from the fire that reflected on each of his friend's faces. "I'm glad you guys came with me on this journey, but I'm still battling the guilt of risking your lives. This is nothing like I expected."

Arrie leaned over and patted Will's shoulder. "Will, I know what you're saying because, to be honest, I'm scared to death here, but we each made our own decision to come. You aren't responsible for us."

Will shook his head. "But what if one of us dies? What if we all die?"

Porty piped in with, "Arrie already died, but you can feel a little responsible if we all die—just a little, though."

Will chuckled softly, and Arrie and Jules soon laughed with him.

Jules jumped to her feet and opened her mouth to speak.

Porty interrupted. "You're not going to say, 'one for all and all for one' or whatever it is again, are you?"

"Not now." Jules smirked. "Look, I'm the girl here, so I feel like I've had to act extra-brave and not show any fear, but I've been shaking in my musketress boots since we jumped through that wall. But there is also something in me now that feels stronger and braver. I feel like I need to commit to being courageous, even when I'm afraid of the unknown. I feel like I owe it to each of you to stop walking the line but to let go of the fear and trust that we'll be okay."

Arrie reached out his clenched hand to give Jules a fist bump. "You *have* been brave, especially when that Stymph bird ruined your outfit."

Jules swatted at Arrie.

"I'm serious. You've been very brave, and it's given me the courage and will to keep going, even when I honestly just wanted to go home. Thank you."

Jules said, "You're not so bad yourself there, Arrs."

Arrie blushed and smiled back.

Will nodded as he glanced at each of them. "I appreciated it, and if it makes you feel any better, I'm just as terrified as you guys. It's not like worrying about missing a big shot in basketball or striking out on the last at-bat in a baseball game. This is life or death."

Porty, Arrie, and Jules shook their heads and said in unison, "That didn't make us feel any better!" Porty and Arrie jumped up and wrestled Will to the ground while Jules mussed his hair until he gave up.

For several hours, they reminisced about playing make-believe action characters when they were younger, building a tree fort in Jules's yard, cheering each other on in sports, and spending countless hours in Will's attic telling jokes, playing games, having arguments, and sharing dreams. Before long, Porty, Arrie, and Jules curled up near the warm fire and drifted off to sleep. Will, however, remained vigilant.

In the morning, the trees with fruit gave the four musketeers their fill for breakfast and the day's journey ahead. As they walked, the trees thinned out, and the friends felt more exposed, less protected than in the forest's darkness. The forest gave way to a swampy area where they had to maneuver through a barren marsh. They decided not to risk drinking the water or tasting the odd prickly berries on the few bushes they passed.

As they slogged onward, the swamp grew thicker and darker. The damp and raw air carried a foul odor, and eerie sounds in the distance gave them all a sense of anxiety and panic.

The tiny fairies lighting their way dwindled in numbers until none remained. Will spun around, unsure where they had come from, much less which direction they should go.

Porty turned with Will. "I really don't like this."

The wind carried a faint voice. "I can help you. I can help you."

"Who is it?" Will asked the wind as the others appeared confused.

"I'm the only one here for you," replied the haunting voice through the thick, enfolding, and blinding mist.

"Okay, I don't hear what you obviously hear"—Arrie glanced around, then leveled his gaze on Will—"but that worried look in your eyes tells me this can't be good. We've gotta find a way out of here. Fast!"

Will took a step forward, but then a little voice cried out from somewhere in the grass, "Hey, be careful who you step on."

Will crouched and squinted into the mist.

A moment later, the figure became visible. Stitch stood between thick clusters of scraggly grass.

"Stitch! Where did you come from? Where have you been?"

The friends gathered in a circle and squatted down to greet him.

Stitch smirked. "I've been with you. I told you to be careful about trusting anyone, didn't I? Was I right?"

"I can't tell you how glad we are to see you." Jules smiled at their little elf-like friend. "This place is the worst, and we don't know how to get out of here."

Stitch tilted his head to the side. "Not to worry. We can get you whatever you need."

"We?" Will peered through the thick mist at nearby clumps of grass, not finding anyone else.

"Sure. I told you I was a Kiggle, right?"

"Yeah. Are there more of you?"

Before Stitch answered, more than a dozen Kiggles almost identical to him stepped forward from the fog. "Meet my friends." Stitch grinned and lifted a hand. "We can help you with anything you need."

Will reached into the pouch and drew out the leather-bound book. "This book has guided us, but it doesn't say anything about this place or where we go next."

Stitch jumped backward. "Don't trust that book. It's full of deception. It will lure you in just to trap you in a place like this." Stitch reached out with his little hands. "Can I take a look?"

Opening the book to the last page message, Will turned the book toward Stitch.

In your darkest moment, do not doubt. I will always be with you. Even when you think I have abandoned you.

Stitch shook his head. "Hah! See? '*I* will always be with you.'" Stitch glanced at each of them. "But you've been abandoned and left to figure things out on your own. Haven't you felt abandoned? This book is full of deception and lies. But we know someone who can help you get what you need and ensure your safety."

"Who's that? Where's this person?" Tired of the riddles and games, Will's patience wore thin.

"We can show you to him. He rules this land and can give you everything you want if you honor him alone," said Stitch.

"What does that mean?"

Stitch reached out for the book. "Can I look closer?"

Will began to hand him the book, but as he peered into Stitch's eyes, he saw an unsettling red glow in them. He yanked the notebook back and hugged it to his chest. "Maybe later, Stitch." Stepping back, Will glanced toward his partners. Suspicion lurked in their eyes.

In the next instant, Stitch's eyes brightened, and his body grew in size, transforming into a large translucent creature with long gray hair and a wrinkled face. He now wore a scarlet red cloak and hat. The other Kiggles changed, too, but they turned into flying creatures with red capes. They filled the sky, floating freely around the friends with a haunting humming sound.

Panic struck Will.

Porty groaned. Arrie shot glances in every direction above them. Jules grabbed Will's arm and drew him toward the others. The group of friends again stood back-to-back in a tight circle.

"Don't be afraid, Will. We can help you. Just trust us," hissed the voice.

Will huddled with Jules, Porty, and Arrie. He whispered, "These are no Kiggles. These look like the Fear Dearies Beno warned us about."

One of the caped creatures swooped down and knocked Jules hard to the ground.

Angered by the attack, Will swung his sword at the

ghost-like figure.

Two came in, lifting Arrie from his crouch and carrying him some fifteen feet in the air. Jules regained her footing and glanced all around them. Demons appeared from the heavy mist and made flying passes at her, screeching with hideous sounds. Jules swung her sword at one and another, then she ducked to avoid a third.

Porty screamed, "Where's Arrie?" but before anyone could answer, several Fear Dearies lifted him from his stance and whisked him away, screaming, "Help!"

Will stood back-to-back with Jules, both of them holding their swords out, fearfully praying for an end to the attacks. "I'll try to strike at their hearts to see if it will stop them," yelled Will.

As a Fear Dearie swooped toward Jules, Will leaped into its path and plunged the tip of his sword into its chest. His blade met with no resistance as if the Fear Dearies were made of thin air, but Will was knocked to the ground.

Two others dove down and grabbed hold of Jules, who gazed down at Will, and as they whisked her away, she yelled, "His ego!"

Will reached up to grab her leg, but she was gone. And the same creature was now swooping in again.

Ego? Ego? Will asked himself in a panic.

His grandfather had often warned him about following his ego. *Follow your heart, Will. That is where your true self exists. Do not follow your ego.* Grandfather would tap the side of his head. *Your ego can easily be puffed up with a false sense of self-importance.*

The Ego. The ego is in your head!

Just as the creature reached down to grab hold of him, Will swung this sword across its neck, cutting off its head.

The body of the Fear Dearie dropped to the ground. Smoke escaped it as it shriveled up before him. Swinging around, Will took off the heads of two more as they attacked, and then a sudden chill and emptiness filled the air.

Something was still nearby.

Will turned in circles, squinting into the damp mist of the dark swamp.

"Donovan!" yelled a breathy voice, sounding impatient and angry. "You—*ssssss*—are not playing gamess-s-s-s here. I can kill you by just thinking it, which would be painful. I have your friends-s-s-s."

"Where are they?" demanded Will.

"Oh, so you care about them now, do you?" breathed the voice.

The thick fog wrapped itself around Will. "I've always cared about them!"

"Is that s-s-s-so? I think you really care more about yourself, putting them in danger that you could s-s-s-stop. Wishing your brother gone when you could find him s-s-s-safe."

Will's head pounded, his heart clenched, and his mind raced. "You know where Sam is?" he shouted in desperation. "Is he alive?"

"I can give you anything, and I can give you back your friends-s-s-s and your annoying little brother s-s-s-safely. That is not a problem—haaaaaa—*sssssss.* You must only put them ahead of yourself and not be s-s-s-so s-s-s-selfish."

Will dropped his shoulders and pleaded, "What do I need to do? Tell me."

"Yes-s-s-s. It is always better to put others before ourselves-s-s-s, isn't it? All you need to do is to s-s-s-show me a little respect. Bow down before me and renounce any other power. It's s-s-s-s-simple, and your reward will be great. You will save your friends-s-s-s- and S-S-S-Sam."

Utterly alone, frightened, and shaking, Will tried to figure out what to do. *Don't think of myself. What should I do? Is the message in the book wrong? If someone is always at my side, where is he now? Can the Giver help?* He continued to turn, searching for the specter. "You can guarantee me they'll be safe?"

The hissing sounded close, almost next to Will's ear. "I can give you anything you want. Anything. I ask for very little in return."

The voices in Will's head seemed to multiply, confusing him. And the air grew colder, the swamp darker in the thickening mist. *What do I do? Whom do I trust? I can't leave them in danger.* He clutched the pouch tighter and reached in to feel the notebook inside. At that moment, he didn't need to pull out the notebook to see what was written inside. "Why would I ever trust anything you say?" he shouted to the specter. "You've tried to kill us. You've lied, and you take—you don't give." Will crouched, his gaze searching, and yelled, "Get away!" Then he waited for an attack, but none came.

In the next moment, he could no longer discern the presence of the specter. The heavy mist lifted, and the light shone all around. Maybe he would find a way out of the desolate swamp by himself.

Chapter 8

While exhausted from the ordeal, a sense of peace settled inside Will as he plodded from the swamp onto more solid ground. Alone and not sure what to do, he scanned his new surroundings. Well-spaced trees grew on the land sloping to his left, and rolling hills stretched to his right. Where could they have taken his friends? Would he ever find Sam?

With no signs around to help him, he slid his hand into the pouch. His fingers brushed the leather-bound book, giving him comfort and the sense that he was not really alone. No matter how it seemed. He drew the book out, opened it to the next page, and read a new message.

You have faced difficult tests and are proving yourself to be strong and trusting.

The journey, however, remains long and will require more than you think you have to give. Keep to what is true and good. Continue to resist the darkness and the allure of power. Know who you are and why you are here—and remain vigilant at all times.

Strengthened by the words, he stuffed the book back into the pouch and continued on his way.

"Hey," said a muffled voice coming from the pouch. Will looked inside.

Stitch stood next to the book, glaring up at him with both hands on his hips. "I warned you to be careful when you shove things back into this pouch, didn't I?"

Will froze, yanked the strap from his shoulder, and held the pouch at arm's length. "How do I know it's you? Or how do I know if you were ever you, if you know what I mean?"

Stitch climbed out, dropped to the ground, then cupped

his chin and squinted. "Not really following, but we don't have time for chit-chat. We have to keep on the move."

Will surveyed the land in front of them. "I have no idea what direction to take. Do you?"

Stitch didn't respond. He just tapped the side of his face, still squinting up at him.

"Yeah, okay." Will sighed. Stitch couldn't guide him. He alone needed to determine the direction of his journey. Maybe if he ... Will reached into the pouch again and wrapped his fingers around the book inside. He tried concentrating, hoping an answer or direction would come.

Nothing.

Maybe he should seek the answer in the book. He glanced at Stitch to see if he agreed, but Stitch only smiled. Will withdrew the leather book and opened it to the last words he had read. He turned the page and stared at the blank page for a long time. Then, without thinking, he blurted, "Please, show me the way."

At the bottom of the page, a line appeared. As the line stretched out, other drawings formed on the page: symbols and markings like on a map. The line wound its way upward through a valley, across a river, and into the hills where the name Eppita appeared. Will glanced back at Stitch. "Should we trust the book?"

Stitch tilted his head. "Why wouldn't we?"

"I was just checking to see if it was you."

Stitch stood with a hand on each hip, tightening his brow in disappointment.

Will chuckled. "Hey, you told me not to trust anyone, didn't you?"

Stitch rolled his eyes and jumped back into the pouch. "Let's go."

Will started down the trail feeling unsure of almost everything. Though, having Stitch with him, he was no longer alone. But he couldn't help thinking about the loneliness he'd experienced as a child—before he had met Arrie, Porty, and Jules and when Sam was too young to play. He remembered longing for a father, someone to teach him things about life or sports, to make him feel safe—and loved. Right now, at this moment, he did not feel safe or loved, only disoriented and confused.

As he reached the crest of a hill, he paused, overcome with awe at the sight of the lush green valley below with a river winding through it. Hope filled him. This resembled the trail the book had shown him. By the time he climbed down and reached the riverbank, the setting sun had turned the sky pink. He would need to find a spot to camp for the night.

Will reached into the pouch, lifted Stitch out and set him on the palm of his hand. "I think we need to stop and get a fire going before we lose the sunlight."

Stitch vigilantly scanned the land around them before nodding in agreement. "I think this will work." He folded his arms across his chest and shivered. "And I think a fire would be a good idea."

The roaring fire brought warmth to the two travelers, light to the pitch-black darkness of the valley, and a peaceful crackle to the quiet of the night. Stitch's face glowed as he stared into the flickering flames.

Will studied his tiny companion's expression. "Stitch?"

Stitch turned. "What is it, Will?"

"I don't really know anything about you other than your name and that you're a Ka . . . Kaggle, right?"

A broad smile spread across Stitch's face. "And shall I call you W-a-ll?"

"It's Will."

"And I'm a Kiggle," replied Stitch.

"Sorry. I'll remember. Do Kiggles have families?"

"Of course," Stitch retorted.

Will's face burned with his embarrassment. "Do you have a family?"

Stitch stared into the flames for several seconds. "I do, but I haven't seen them in a long, long time."

"Where are they? What happened?"

Stitch stood up his full six inches and turned to Will. "Hundreds of people from my village, including my wife and children, were taken to various towns as captives to provide diversion and entertainment for children and bored spouses."

Will leaned down to make eye contact with Stitch. "I'm sorry. I didn't know. That is so wrong. Do you know where they are? Can we get them back?"

Stitch half-smiled as if recognizing Will's sincerity. "Will Donovan, you are looking for your family, and I am looking for mine. Let's just say that we are on this quest together, and I feel more hopeful than I have in a long time that I might see them again."

Will smiled and nodded, putting out his finger for Stitch to grasp both his hands as a sign of agreement and solidarity. Will lay down on the grassy floor of the riverbank. "I'm feeling a little more hopeful myself." Then, his eyes closed for the night.

Chapter 9

The morning sun woke Will from his deep slumber, and he rubbed his eyes as he scanned the area and the ashy remains of last night's fire. Where was Stitch? After frantically checking the pouch and the area around him, he stood up and began searching for him.

He found the tiny Kiggle standing across the riverbank as if pondering how to cross. "Stitch, I thought I had lost you again. It looks like a long way to cross."

"Hmm," replied Stitch, scratching his head. "There's no wood in the area large enough to build a raft."

"What should we do? The map in the book shows us crossing the river to get to Eppita," Will said, squinting. Stitch remained quiet as Will scoured the area for anything that might float for a crossing. When he turned back, he had to rub his eyes. *Am I seeing what I think I'm seeing?*

Stitch was almost halfway across the river, walking on top of the water.

Will cupped his hands to his mouth. "Stitch! Stitch! How did you do that? I didn't know you could do magic."

Stitch raised his hand but kept his head down. "Come on!" He waved Will in his direction.

"Sorry, but not even my mother thinks I can walk on water. What do I do?"

Stitch continued to wave Will onward.

Shaking his head, Will asked, "Is this one of those trust things? Will I be able to do it if I just trust?"

Stitched yelled back, "I told you not to trust anyone, but you can trust the rocks in the water. Just carefully step from stone to stone!"

He studied the river but only saw water. With one foot

securely on land, Will stepped out, feeling around for something solid. There it was. His trust grew, and the rocks became visible as he stepped from one to another until he reached Stitch. "Why are we stopping in the middle?"

"Well, my legs are too short to reach the next stone, so I thought I might hitch a ride."

Will smiled, picked up Stitch, and stepped carefully from stone to stone until they reached the opposite embankment safely.

It was another day's journey before they reached the mountain's crest that overlooked a city below. The light of the day faded as they searched for a good spot to camp for the night. "I hope that's Eppita below us." Will peered up into the night sky.

"You're looking at the bright star above the city?"

"Yeah. It's much brighter than the others. I remember seeing one like it several days ago. I think it was when we met Beno."

"Who's Beno?"

"He, ah—he's Beno." Will shrugged. "When we first saw him, we thought he was a rock. Then he turned into a funny-looking creature and said he was a Lydian or something like that."

"Hmm. I haven't seen a star like this before, but you've seen two. I wonder if that means something."

Will found a comfortable grassy spot and sat down. "I don't know, but I'm ready to call it a night. We can head down into the city in the morning. I wish I knew what to expect, but I'm hoping Sam is there—and Jules, Arrie, and Porty too."

Realizing he'd just blurted out a wish, he snapped his gaze to his hands. Phew. He hadn't touched the goblet when he'd said it. Who knew how many wishes they would need as the journey progressed? Maybe after finding everyone, they'd need them to get home.

Will stretched out on the grass. The book had led him to Eppita for a reason. Maybe he'd find them all there.

Closing his eyes, sleep came quickly, but troubled dreams soon rushed in.

Will raced down the street with his friends while Sam called for him and tried to keep up. Sam seemed desperate to show his big brother something he was proud of, but Will only ran faster. He had no interest in wasting time on his little brother's silly accomplishments. When he turned to see how far behind Sam was, Will panicked. He couldn't see him anywhere. Suddenly, a ball of fire shot across his path. It came from the fire-breathing Chimera, who glared at him with menacing eyes and held Sam in his clutches. "Leave him alone!" shouted Will. "Leave him alone!"

Something touched Will's cheek, pulling him from his dream. Will shook his head and swatted whatever had touched him. More awake now, he opened his eyes and saw Stitch lying flat on his backside. "What happened?"

Stitch stood up and brushed himself off. "Don't ask me. I think you had a bad dream, and I was trying to wake you up. I'll know better next time."

He sat up to make sure Stitch was okay. "I'm sorry. Did I hurt you?"

Stitch smiled. "Not to worry. Kiggles are pretty resilient."

Both Will and Stitch turned their attention to the rising sun on the horizon and the spectacular colors that began to paint the sky, everything from golden yellow to shades of pink and purple. The city of Eppita lay below them, and neither knew what to expect from the day ahead. With

Stitch safely in the pouch, and still unsettled by his dream, Will descended the steep hill and reached the road. In a matter of minutes, he approached the open gate of the protective stone wall that encompassed the city. Hordes of people entered the gates with carts of produce and wares for a market.

Will stopped. Would they shun an outsider like him? He reached into the pouch for Stitch.

In a hushed tone, Stitch said, "No. Leave me here in case someone wants to take me for their plaything. I can't chance it."

Taking a deep breath, Will entered through the high-arched gate. The market square in front of him bustled with activity as merchants set up their carts and tents for the day's market. Suddenly, Will felt a tug on the strap of the pouch slung over his shoulder.

"How much for the leather bag?" asked an old woman, running her hand over the leather. "I'll give you two dracels for it—in cash!" Hunched over, her skin wrinkled, and a large wart on one cheek that was hard to ignore, the old woman tugged on the pouch. She wore a broad-brimmed hat and cloak of worn, thick, coarse cloth.

Will stood frozen, clutching the pouch with both hands.

"Well, are you going to sell it or not?" she gruffed.

Shaking his head, Will backed away, signaling the value of his possession.

"I'll give you five for it," ventured the old woman, squinting her eyes.

He continued to shake his head, then he turned from her. Racing to escape the old woman and not watching ahead, he bumped into someone and landed with a thud.

A young girl close to his own age stood gaping down at him.

Holding onto the pouch, Will scrambled back to his feet. "I'm sorry. Are you okay?"

The girl smirked and brushed off one sleeve of her long dress. "It would take more than that to do me in."

The girl was pretty, and Will felt a flush work its way across his face, the girl standing over him.

With her chin up, confidence showed in her piercing blue eyes and the tilt of her head. She wore her long blond hair in a braid that fell over her shoulder.

A bit thrown off by her beauty, Will stammered, "Um. I'm just glad you're okay. Is this the town of Eppita?"

"You're new here?" She raised a brow, seeming more curious now, and offered her right hand. "I'm Leata. Any chance you have a name?"

Will shook her hand, his face flushing. "I'm Will, and this is—um, yeah, I'm Will."

Leata narrowed her eyes. "Are there more of you?"

"No, no. Well, I had three friends with me, but I lost them in the wilderness."

Leata's eyebrows drew together, and her face paled. "I'm so sorry. Why did you come to Eppita?"

Will hesitated, thinking of the map in the leather book. "I don't know. I'm just trying to find them—and my brother. My friends were helping me to find my brother."

With half a smile, Leata said, "I'm sorry, but you're not doing so well, are you?"

Eyes squinted, Will stared down, feeling a sense of hopelessness about finding Sam.

Leata's smile disappeared. "Look, maybe I can help you. How long have you been in the barren land? Have you eaten?"

Will shook his head, his stomach rumbling as he thought of food.

"Come with me," Leata said, already three paces ahead.

Will glanced down into the pouch and whispered, "What should I do?"

"Follow her," Stitch answered back from the bottom of the pouch. "Do you have any better ideas?"

Will shrugged and ran to catch up to Leata. Breathing heavily, he kept pace with her. They wound their way through a maze of streets lined with buildings and small piazzas. As they turned a corner, Will paused to marvel at the size of an ancient-looking edifice with tall, fluted columns and figures of animals and people carved into the triangular stone pediment at the top of the building. "What is this?"

Leata peered up at the building she probably now took for granted. "It's an ancient temple. People used to worship false gods here. I heard that once the nation was whole, people stopped believing in false spirits and myths and came to know and love the Giver."

Will ascended the steep stone steps and touched the large, heavy column. "What happened?"

"I don't know. People here were—still are—hardworking, good, and honest, for the most part, but they lost something along the way. Some say that the people of Eppita lost their love and passion for the Giver and started putting their own wishes first. They stopped trusting in him and started coming here again, thinking they could find better answers to their problems."

Will turned to Leata. "Have you ever been inside?"

Leata shook her head. "There is a deceitful one who preys on people's fears. The people of Eppita have endured hardships for many years, and he tries to get them to look to him for the answers that never seem to come. I've never had a good feeling about this temple."

Will glanced up at the tall columns, intrigued by Leata's distrust. Then, he remembered his frightening encounters in the wilderness with what could be described as nothing but evil and deceitful. "Why do people come here then?"

Leata strode away from the building. "I don't know. We've had nothing but hard times since people began worshiping here. I think he gets in people's heads, promising them a better answer. Let's not talk about it. We're almost at my home."

Chapter 10

Down a few more streets, Leata stopped at the door of a modest-looking home and opened it. "Anybody home?" she yelled, but no one responded. Will started to enter, but she put her hand out. "No boys allowed when no one's home."

Will opened his mouth as if shocked but didn't question the house rules. On the porch, he sat and waited on a stone bench while she disappeared inside.

A few minutes later, Leata brought a plate with orange slices and a sandwich for Will. "I'm sure you're hungry."

Will didn't argue as he slid over on the stone bench for Leata to sit. He snatched up the sandwich and took a huge bite.

Leata laughed.

"What's so funny?" Will said with his full mouth.

"Eating like that, you're going to choke to death before you ever find your friends and brother. What's your brother's name?"

"Sam. He's only ten." Using a little self-restraint, Will finished his mouthful before he popped in an orange slice.

"You must be frantic searching for him. How long has he been lost?"

Will thought for several seconds. "It's been a few days, but it seems like a lot longer."

Leata sighed. "My dad has been gone for years now, and my sister—"

"You have a sister?"

Leata nodded as she twisted her braid in her fingers. "Tivona. She's seven years older than me. She lost the boy she loved—well, he's a man now— years ago."

Will discreetly dropped breadcrumbs and pieces of meat from his sandwich into the pouch for Stitch as Leata talked. "If he was her true love, why would he leave her?"

"We don't know. She says she doesn't love him anymore, but I can tell she's never stopped loving him even if he has forsaken her."

"That's sad," said Will as a young woman approached them.

"What's sad?" the woman stopped a short distance away. She wore her long brown hair tied to one side with a blue bow.

Will felt himself blush, captivated by her striking beauty.

Leata smiled at Will's blushing response, then glanced up at the young woman. "Tivona, you're home. This is Will, er . . ."

"Donovan. Will Donovan. Are you Leata's sister?"

Tivona nodded.

"She was good enough to offer me some food after a long journey."

Tivona gave Will a look of inspection as if to see if she could trust him with her younger sister. "Journey? Where are you coming from?"

Will hesitated. How much of his story should he share? Certain he could trust Leata, he decided to trust Tivona as well. "I'm searching for my younger brother. I came with three friends across the wilderness, and now I've lost them as well."

Tivona's eyes snapped open wide, and she jerked back. "I haven't heard of anyone who's survived that barren wasteland. Is it not as dangerous as they say?"

Will winced, the image of a Fear Dearie flitting through his mind. "It is dangerous, but we had no choice. I'm hoping someone in Eppita can help me find my brother and friends."

Tivona opened the door to their home. "Come in. Do you have any clues as to where they may be?"

Will shook his head and stepped onto a braided rug just inside the door. A narrow staircase rose in front of him, and warm light came from one of the rooms off to one side.

Tivona moved into the sunny kitchen on the right, where a colorful bowl of fruit sat on a wooden table. "Hmm. There's someone we can ask. I don't know how much he can help us, but we can try."

Leata motioned Will into a room on the left, a sitting room with an overstuffed sofa and a comfortable-looking leather chair by the fireplace. She leaned in and whispered, "Will, I think that was hard for her."

"What was hard?" Will furrowed his brow.

"I believe she's going to take you to see Jobin. He has an unusual gift for seeing outside these walls—knowing when trouble is coming to the city or where the lost may be found." Leata's gaze dropped, then shifted toward the little hallway to the kitchen. "But when it came to our father and then to Tivona's lost love, he couldn't offer any help. She lost hope, and it sent her into a very dark period. I'm surprised she would return to him for a stranger."

Will stared down at the worn, uneven floorboards. Desperation rose inside. He needed guidance, or even a single clue as to what to do next. He was guided to this city for a reason, and Jobin might be that reason. He took a deep breath and sighed. "She doesn't have to go if you can tell me where to find him."

"That's the problem. No one knows where he lives now

except for Tivona."

Will got up and stepped into the kitchen, the floorboards creaking under his boots.

Tivona turned at the sound of his steps, holding a steaming teapot.

"Tivona, I have to ask . . . why are you doing this? Why are you willing to help me when you don't even know me?"

Before Tivona could respond, a faint voice said in a frustrated tone, "Let her help you!"

Tivona's eyebrows furrowed, and her gaze shot to the pouch hanging from his shoulder. "Why is your pouch moving?"

"It's nothing." Will clutched the pouch, almost wishing he'd left it in the other room.

"Let me see it." Tivona stepped toward him, reaching with one hand.

"I can't. Sorry." Will backed up, tucking the pouch under his arm.

"Then I can't help you."

The voice came again. "Don't be stupid. Let her help you."

"Shhhh." Will squeezed the pouch. Stitch punched back, his little fists making the pouch seem to come alive. Giving up, Will rolled his eyes and let out a weary sigh. "I guess you don't need protecting then, huh?" Will opened the pouch, reached inside, and scooped the active little creature into the palm of his hand. He lifted him into view of Tivona and Leata.

Tivona's eyes widened as she approached the new stranger. "Oh, wow. They are real."

"Of course I'm real." Stitch planted his hands firmly on his hips.

"No offense intended. I've heard of these very small creatures. I think they were called, um, Kagglits?"

Rolling his eyes, Stitch said, "Kiggles. Why can't you people keep a simple name straight? Kiggles."'

"Kiggle," repeated Tivona. "I am truly sorry. I'll remember it always." She gave him a genuine smile and extended her pinky finger in a welcoming manner.

Reaching out, Stitch said, "Sorry for being defensive. It gets a little monotonous in this pouch after a while. You said you know where another Kiggle might be?"

"I heard about a family that gave a small creature to their daughter for a present. I think it was in Sumara," Tivona said.

Stitch glanced up at Will. "We have to go there. Maybe that's why we were led to this city?"

Will nodded. "Okay, but I need to find out if there's any information about Sam or my friends here." He turned to Tivona. "Would you tell me how to find this Jobin?"

Tivona glanced toward her sister and then placed her hand on Will's shoulder. "I will take you there after sunset."

Leata smiled at her sister with a look of both admiration and concern.

As the sun set and the streets were lit by torches on the doorways, Tivona led Will and Leata through a winding maze of roads until they reached the door of a modest stone cottage. Tivona knocked with a rhythmic pattern but received no reply.

As minutes passed, disappointment crept into Will's being, but he remained quiet and patient.

Tivona knocked on the door again, this time with three delayed taps.

Two taps came in response!

She knocked on the door once more with a single tap. Suddenly, the door creaked open to let in the evening visitors.

Inside, an old man held an oil lantern to see each of their faces while he remained in the dark behind his hooded cloak. As the light moved, it fell onto the old man's face, revealing a sunken, scarred area where one of his eyes should be. "What are you looking for?" the man grunted.

"We seek Jobin's advice," Tivona replied.

"For what purpose?"

"This boy has lost his brother and friends. He needs to find them and hopes they aren't in danger."

The old man held his lantern to Will's face, studying it more intently. He grunted, "Why do you think you can get help here?"

Tivona's face fell, and she pressed her hands together. "Please, sir, he has traveled a long distance through the wilderness to reach Eppita and seek Jobin's help."

The old man grumbled something under his breath. Then he motioned the visitors to follow him and opened the door to a long, dimly lit hallway. A massive wooden door stood at the end of the dark passageway, men on each side guarding it. The old man motioned for them to open the door.

Will reached for the cold brass doorknob and turned it. Heart pounding with his anxiety, he shoved the heavy door open to a large, dark room. Then he peered inside at a shadowy figure seated on a carved wooden chair.

The wheezy voice of a man with a foreign accent broke a moment of silence. "Who are you?"

Will turned to Tivona, whose face was lit only by the faint light of the old man's lantern.

She nodded to Will.

"I-I am Will Donovan."

"From where do you come?" the strange man said.

He wished he could see the man rather than talk to a figure in the shadows as his gut twisted with anxiety and hope. "I'm from America. Somehow, my brother disappeared through the wall in our attic, and my friends and I passed through the same wall to find him. I have no clue where he's gone, and now I've lost my friends too. We're here to seek your help."

A faint shadowy light shifted, revealing the face of the man. His head was bald, his nose prominent and pointed, and his eyes seemed mysteriously dark. He extended a gnarled hand and motioned Will closer with his long fingers. "I know of only a few people from that place. What is the name of the brother you seek?"

Will shuffled forward, uncertainty building. "My brother's name is Sam. He's only ten years old."

Jobin squinted. "You come not alone, do you?"

"No, but my friends have disappeared too."

Jobin shook his head. "No, you do not come here to me alone."

Will glanced back at Tivona and Leata. "They were kind enough to bring me."

"I'm not referring to them. You have not come alone, have you?" persisted Jobin.

"Ahh—" Will shook his head, not sure what the man meant.

"If I were to look in that satchel of yours, what would I find?"

He hesitated to respond. Panic overcame him, his heart thumping out of control and sweat gathering on his brow, but he worked to react calmly. He didn't want to put Stitch at risk.

"You want me to help you, but you can't be honest with me?"

Will had no reply. He just stood there trembling inside.

"You are conflicted, are you not? Can you be loyal to your brother, your friends, *and* your companion? Whom do you choose when you must choose?"

Will searched his mind for an answer, but then the pouch shifted and moved under his arm. Stitch had made his way to the top of the pouch, and now he poked his head out and shouted, "He's only trying to protect me."

Jobin tilted his head, an amused smile flickering on his face. "What tiny creature is this now?"

Stitch flung one arm in the air. "I'm a Kiggle. Can't you just help the kid find his brother?"

With his eyes fixed on Stitch, Jobin motioned Will closer. "I've heard stories about these tiny creatures. There are more of them. Hmm. To answer your question, I may be able to help the boy, but I don't know if that would be wise."

His hope deflating, Will blurted, "Why? Why won't you help?"

Leata tugged on Will's shirt to stop him from pushing Jobin's patience too far.

Jobin sighed. "I can tell you that your brother is alive but not safe. I am still getting no signs about your friends, but I sense that danger follows you. I sympathize with your situation, but I must put the welfare of Eppita first."

Tivona squeezed her hands together. "Jobin, what does that mean?"

"Eppita once was part of a great and noble kingdom, now scattered and broken. I sense that something significant will soon happen and that we face an important judgment, possibly another significant punishment for losing our way. We were once a beacon of loyalty and goodness." He turned to Will. "You have come from the wilderness where the evil one resides. Few have survived that journey, and I don't know if you are to be trusted. You weren't honest about your friend; I don't know if he is a sign of bad things for Eppita." Jobin motioned the guards toward Will and Stitch. "Take them away."

Tivona pleaded with Jobin. "We came here for your help. I don't believe Will is a danger to Eppita. He is a young boy!"

"Tivona, we are approaching a fight for our survival as a people. You have only just met this young man and do not know him. We're dealing with the deceitful one; his ways can seem good when they are not. I can't take that chance based on what I've heard. I ask you and your sister to leave now and forget what you've heard."

The door opened, and guards ushered Will, Stitch, Tivona, and Leata out. As she neared the doorway, Tivona turned back to Jobin and snapped her words. "You abandoned my father and someone I loved because you were afraid. I came to you for help, not cowardice."

Jobin didn't respond, and the door closed on Tivona and Leata.

Chapter 11

One of the guards led Will down several flights of stairs to a dark cell with no windows or visible way to escape. Another guard locked Stitch in a small cage that might have been used to keep small animals. Will sat on the hard bed with his hands over his head, panic and hopelessness warring inside him. Instead of gaining valuable clues to find Sam, Jules, Arrie, and Porty, he had become a prisoner, stuck in a cell for who knows how long. Would they execute him if Jobin believed he was truly a danger to the city?

Fortunately, they didn't confiscate his pouch, so when no guards were watching, Will pulled out the leather book to see if he could find help. The last page still showed the map directing him to Eppita. Before his eyes, a line appeared, drawing a path from Eppita to the town of Sumara, the one Tivona had mentioned. She thought a Kiggle family might have been taken there.

Laughing to himself, Will shook his head. *A lot of good that's going to do us in here. How do we travel to Sumara when we are locked up?* In the next instant, words appeared next to the extended path: *Trust and Loyalty.*

Not understanding the point and still weighed down with defeat, Will set the book aside.

Sometime later, two guards came to the cell and unlocked the door. "Come with us," one said. They escorted Will into a room with Jobin, leaving Stitch behind in his small wire cage.

Will hesitated to look up at the imposing figure in the shadows. Apprehension welled in his chest as he stood alone with Jobin in the dark room.

"I know you think I'm being harsh and unsympathetic

to your situation, but I need to protect the people here," said Jobin in his gravelly voice, shifting slightly to look more closely at the boy.

Will finally glanced up, finding his eyes more accustomed to the dim light. "I understand, but I promise you I'm no threat."

Jobin stared at Will for a long moment, his dark eyes seeming to assess Will. "If you can give me your word of honor, I will let you continue your search. You must leave Eppita immediately and never be the cause of any harm to her."

Relief flooded Will, and he wanted to shout for joy, but he controlled himself and simply said, "Thank you, Jobin. I give you my word of honor."

Jobin nodded. "You can leave by that door, and someone will take you outside the gates."

Will turned to the door but then paused. "I'll just need to get my companion, Stitch, before I go."

Jobin signaled to the guard. "You must leave without him. These tiny creatures could be the tools of the Taker—a spy or something. I can't take that chance. I need to observe him longer to know his true nature."

Will's shoulders slumped, and he sighed deeply. *Why is this so hard? What do I do?*

"Why do you hesitate, Will Donovan?" Jobin tilted his head, still gazing at Will with his dark, curious eyes. "Surely this tiny creature that you only just met, nothing more than a plaything, isn't more important than your blood brother and lifelong friends?"

Will thought about the truth in Jobin's words, but he couldn't get himself to move. Stitch had been his guide and was searching for his own family, looking to rescue them from their prisons. He couldn't abandon him in that cage any more than he could risk leaving Sam alone in danger. "I can't leave him. It's not right."

Jobin squinted at him as if intrigued by Will's answer. "You are a very loyal friend, but is that loyalty worth your brother's life and the safety of your friends?"

Will didn't respond.

"So be it; you can rejoin this friend you are so devoted to. I cannot risk the safety of Eppita." Jobin waved his hand, motioning for the guard to bring Will back to his cell, where Stitch awaited him.

As the steel door slammed shut, Stitch clung to the bars of his tiny cage. "Are you okay? What happened?"

Will sat down on the bed and sighed. "I'm okay, but I think Jobin is testing me or something. We need to get out of here."

Stitch tapped his chin. "If this guy is some sort of wise man or has special powers to see things, why doesn't he know that you're not a danger to Eppita and let you go? It makes no sense. I know he is suspicious of me, but it should be easy to read that you're no threat. Did you try to plead with him to leave me and let you go?"

Will's heart melted at the selflessness of his friend. "I wouldn't leave you." He located the latch and pried it open to let Stitch out of the small cage.

"That's much better." Stitch hopped out and paced across the bed, one arm folded across his chest and tapping his head as if trying to concoct a plan. "Wait a minute."

"What?"

"He didn't offer to let you go without me, did he? Don't tell me that."

Will didn't respond.

Stitch gazed up at him, his eyes softened at Will's

sacrifice and loyalty.

Sleep came slowly on the hard mattress in the damp cell, but eventually, Stitch dozed off, and Will fell into a deep sleep. A sudden metallic bang jolted Will awake in the wee hours of the night. Quickly, he sat upright in bed.

The sound seemed to come from the large bolt on the door.

Will's heart fluttered in panic. He rolled off the bed and crouched, his breaths coming quick as he watched the door open and two cloaked figures enter the cell in the dark. Will moved to grab the goblet from the pouch when one of the figures shoved her hood back, revealing her identity.

Dressed in a long black cape, Leata stood inside the cell, holding a small lantern that lit her blond hair and smiling face.

Will closed his eyes and sighed with relief. "What are you doing here?" he exclaimed in a hushed tone as Tivona removed her hood.

"We don't have time. Let's go!" Tivona handed Will his pouch. She held a bow in her other hand and wore a quiver full of arrows strapped across her back.

Will jumped up, put the awoken Stitch in the pouch, and slung it across his shoulder. "How did you get by the guards?

Tivona smiled. "My innocent little sister here has a trick to disarm people. It's only temporary. Help me pull these two into the cell."

They dragged the motionless bodies of the two guards into the cell and locked it shut. Then they crept down the dark passageways until they reached the door to the outside.

A relief sentry drew near, his head turning every which

way as if surprised to find no one guarding the door. Before turning toward them, Leata gripped the back of his neck, and he collapsed to the ground.

"You'll have to teach me that sometime." Will helped pull the guard out of sight. After making their way through the maze of streets, they finally reached the gates of Eppita. "I can't thank you enough for rescuing us. I won't forget you."

Leata smiled at her sister and turned back to Will. "I know you won't, and you're not going alone."

Will drew back, stunned. "I can't ask you to go. This is your home, and I don't know what I might run into."

Tivona began walking through the gate. "First of all, you didn't ask, and secondly—"

"We've just helped two criminals to escape," Leata interrupted, "so that makes us outside the law too. Therefore, we have no choice but to go with you."

Will couldn't argue with either point, and he more than appreciated having the company ... wherever this journey would take them. He drew out the leather book again to see the next phase of the map, which led to Sumara. "I guess it's on to Sumara we go. It looks like it should take about a day and a half. Does that sound right?"

Leata pulled her hood up, tightened her cape, and smiled at Will. "I guess we'll find out."

Chapter 12

Tivona led the way, her bow at the ready as she scanned the rocky path ahead for danger from thieves or worse.

Will followed several yards behind with Leata, anticipating the trek through the hills in front of them.

"So, tell me your story, Will Donovan."

"Me? I don't have a story." Will laughed.

"Everyone has a story," replied Leata. "I bet yours is more interesting than you think. How old are you? What is your family like? What do you like to do?"

"Slow down! Slow down! There's nothing special about my life. I'm thirteen, and Sam is ten. My father left home without a word just after Sam was born, so it's just been my mother and us. Now, *she's* something special." Will meant it. He'd taken her for granted most of his life, but Mom worked hard to provide for the family, keep them united, and show her appreciation for Will and Sam.

The look in Leata's eyes showed she recognized his sincerity.

Will's cheeks warmed under her gaze, so he quickly added, "I love to play baseball and basketball."

"What are those?"

"I'll show you sometime. I especially like spending time with my best friends—Jules, Arrie, and Porty." Will choked up a bit. "I just wish I knew where they were."

"So, Mr. Will, how did you end up here?"

"I wish I knew. Actually, I have to stop wishing since that's what got me into trouble. We were dressed up for Halloween—that's a day where kids dress up in costumes and go to people's houses for candy."

Leata eyed Will up and down, then she laughed. "I was

wondering if you actually dressed that way where you come from."

Will had forgotten that he still wore his musketeer outfit. His cheeks really burned now, likely turning beet red. "Ah, no, this was my costume. It would take too long to explain. Well, my brother can be a nuisance, and when he stepped on my candy, I got angry and wished that he would disappear—and he did."

Leata stopped in her tracks. "You have powers to make people disappear? Can you make them reappear?"

"I don't have powers to make anyone disappear, and I obviously can't make them reappear either. I know that's confusing, but trust me. I'm just sick with the thought of never finding Sam."

Leata rested her hand on Will's shoulder and peered into his eyes. "I'm sure you are, but we'll find him. I'm sorry about your father. Mine went off to war when I was little and never came back. I can't even remember what he looked like. He doesn't seem real to me sometimes."

"Do you miss him?"

Leata hesitated and then nodded.

Before Will thought of another question, Tivona spun to face them and motioned for everyone to take cover behind nearby boulders. She stole over to them in a crouching position as they hid.

"What is it?" Will whispered.

"I don't know." Tivona peeked over the boulder. "Rustling sounds keep jumping from side to side, making me worry."

Leata said, "You're making *us* worry. What do you think it might be?"

"I haven't a clue." Tivona gripped her bow and drew an arrow from her full quiver. "Thieves might murder for nothing more than the change in your pocket, but something seems eerily different about this."

Leata peeked around the boulder. "You're spooking us out. How do you know what lives in these hills, anyway?"

Tivona turned to her younger sister. "I went to look for my friend. Mom told you I was visiting with family, but I had set off to find him."

Before Leata could respond, something scraped the ground in front of them. Her eyes widened.

Will took a deep breath and held it. The sisters remained silent as the three hid behind large, jagged rock formations.

The next instant, a tall creature covered in animal skins leaped onto the hard surface above them, and the three jumped back. With long, straggly hair on his head, face, and arms, the creature stood at least seven feet tall and was twice as broad as any normal-sized man. Its fiery eyes showed agitation. While the first creature stood growling at them, a second one jumped up beside him, curling its arms and clenching its fists.

Tivona straightened from her crouched position, backed up several yards, and nocked an arrow on her bow, aiming it at the first creature, ready to defend her companions.

Will drew his sword, and Leata, her machete-like weapon, before joining Tivona in a hopeless attempt to fight these hairy beasts.

The first creature leaped at Tivona just as she loosed an arrow and drew another from her quiver. The arrow pierced the beast's heart, and he dropped with a thud to the ground inches from her feet.

As the second beast readied to attack Will and Leata, another leaped onto the rock formation, three more behind him.

Heart thumping hard against his chest, Will lifted his sword. "We mean you no harm. If this is your land, we will leave."

The creatures growled and grunted even louder, thrashing their arms around.

Will swung his sword from side to side in defense.

"Watch your frantic swings!" Leata aimed her weapon at the second beast. "I don't think these hideous creatures are open to negotiations." She lunged with her machete-like weapon, forcing the nearest creature back.

Tivona loosed another arrow just as the second beast soared toward Leata, wounding him but not causing him to retreat.

Another beast came from behind the friends, swiping his sharp-clawed paws at them.

With the others busy fighting, Will took on this new threat. Using every ounce of strength and skill, he swung—landing a sharp blow to its arm—and then swung again—striking its shoulder.

Wailing sounds filled the air. The beast fell. Two more beasts also fell, the result of Leata and Tivona's skilled attacks. But as those three went down, others emerged from the boulders, descending on the friends. One clutched a hefty, jagged rock and reared back, his eyes locked on Will's head.

Leata swung her weapon at his neck with a weary grunt and dropped him to the ground. Tivona stopped two others in their tracks with deadly shots, then motioned to Will in a warning.

Will twisted to see what approached, and his heart sank. Two almost flanked him—and he swung and lunged to ward them off—but dozens lumbered toward them—more beasts than they could ever handle. One struck Leata with a forceful blow that sent her hard to the ground, and another grabbed Tivona's bow from her hand.

Without a thought, Will reached his free hand into the pouch and felt around until he touched metal. Then he whispered, "I wish we were invisible until this was over!"

With those words, the beasts paused, shock coloring their expressions as they swung aimlessly about. Their grunting lessened, and confused, questioning sounds replacing it. Soon, the creatures stopped fighting altogether, and turned to look all around. One motioned to the others as if trying to determine where their three intended victims had gone. They apparently could not see Will or his friends at all. The confused beasts moved out a minute later, peering at the ground and to either side as if trying to track them down.

Chapter 13

Will crouched in the hollowed-out area behind the large rocks. It was now empty and quiet, very quiet. A small stone slid on the sloped surface, and then a piece of gravel rolled down the ledged rock. Once it stopped, a cautious silence filled the space again.

After several moments, a hushed voice whispered, "Tivvy?"

"Are you okay, Leata?"

"I'm okay. Where are you?"

"I was going to ask you the same. Will? Are you there too?"

While the girls' voices came from nearby, Will could not see them. "I'm here," he whispered.

"Are you okay?" asked Leata.

"I think so." Gravel moved again as Will stood up.

"What happened? I can't see either of you."

Will reached out in the direction of Tivona's voice. He touched a hand he could not see and pulled her to her feet.

"What sort of magic is this?" she asked.

"It was me." A bit of regret niggled through Will's mind. "I panicked and wished we were invisible."

At this point, Will sensed Leata next to him.

In a still hushed tone, she exclaimed, "What are you—a wizard or something?"

"Don't I wish." Will chuckled. "I lost hope when those hairy things started to show up in numbers. Hopefully, they aren't the welcoming committee from Sumara."

The air moved near Will, along with a swooshing sound, as if Leata had tried whacking his shoulder. It happened again and again, and—whoops! She finally found his shoulder.

"Now we know you're a comedian, but you didn't tell us how you covered us with invisible paint."

Will rubbed his shoulder where she'd smacked it, though it didn't really hurt. "It's not paint—oh, never mind. Are you at least happy we escaped?"

"Narrowly," Leata said. "You could've waved your wand before I was knocked to the ground. That hurt!"

More remorse tugged at him. "I need to be careful. I don't know how long this journey will take, and I'm down to six wishes. I think those beasts are long gone now. We should try to make some progress."

"I think you're right," Tivona said, "but I do have one question, Mr. Donovan. Are we going to stay invisible forever?"

Suddenly, despite the seemingly fatal wound, one of the beasts on the ground reached out and managed to grab Will's leg.

Quick footfalls indicated that one of the girls—probably Leata—lunged toward the beast. Then, a whooshing sound filled the air nearby, and the beast's clawed hand separated from its body. The beast drew its last breath. Will exhaled. "Thanks." He turned toward where he guessed Tivona stood. "I don't know the answer to your question, though. I wished we'd vanish until we were safe. I guess I didn't specify safe from what. Maybe we're not out of danger yet."

As they hiked the next leg of the journey, they remained invisible and whispered to each other to ensure they all stayed together. Other than that, they remained quiet to avoid alerting possible spies.

By nightfall, they reached the safety of a forest of tall trees with thick trunks. They did not want to risk lighting a fire, so they covered themselves with green-leafed branches to keep warm in the cool night air. Will glanced up at the majestic trees, wondering if they could move or talk like the trees in the other forest. Not having heard or seen Stitch in a while, he lowered his hand into the pouch to make sure he was still safely inside. "Good night, Stitch."

"Goodnight, Will."

Leata smiled. "Good night, Stitch and Will."

"Goodnight, Mary Ellen," joked Will.

"Mary Ellen?" Leata whispered.

Will chuckled to himself. "Never mind. It was from an old television show and would take too long to explain."

"Television?"

"Sleep well, Leata." Will shook his head, trying to imagine life with no television. "And you too, Tivona. Thank you for coming with me. You saved my life today."

Tivona replied, "I think you saved all of ours."

As the morning sunlight cut through the slitted openings between the trees, Will opened his eyes, feeling rested after a deep sleep. Tivona, awake already, sat nearby with her bow in her hand, and Leata remained sound asleep under the branches. Tivona gripped her bow in one hand and pulled an arrow back as far as possible against the taut string. Her archery form was perfect, and Will stared into the woods to identify her target. The arrow shot through a narrow opening, like thread through the eye of a needle, and finally passed through a small hole in a tree trunk some distance away.

"That would have been an unbelievable shot if you were aiming at that exact spot."

Tivona turned to Will with a half-smile and a wink. Her

quiver always seemed full, regardless of how many arrows she shot.

"Wait a minute!" Will shouted.

Leata sat up at the sound of Will's exclamation. "Hey, I can see you."

Will held his hands out in front of his face and smiled. Then he reached into his pouch, gently lifted Stitch out, and rested him on the forest floor.

"Finally, a bit of fresh air. What's the plan for today?" Stitch yawned and stretched, then stood up and touched his toes.

Pulling the book from his pouch, Will studied the map and noticed the route now went out and around the forest.

Tivona stepped closer and studied the book over his shoulder. "Going around the forest will take us the better part of the day. Straight ahead brings us to Sumara in just a few hours."

Will glanced sideways at Leata, feeling conflicted as he studied the change in the path drawn in the book. "I have to trust the guidance in the book. I think we should go around, as it says."

Tivona placed a hand on one hip and shook her head. "I've been this way before, and straight ahead is the fastest and safest route. I think we should continue with the original plan."

Leata rested her hand on Tivona's shoulder. "Tivvy, we should trust Will. I know it doesn't seem to make sense, but I want to follow his instincts on this."

Stitch nodded. "I think she's right."

"Easy for you to say, little one. You don't have to walk it." Tivona shook her head at Stitch.

After a long, vigilant day of hiking, they finally arrived

on the other side of the forest, and Tivona closed her eyes as she exhaled a sigh of relief. "I guess we avoided that problem." She pointed to where a fire raged at a distant edge of the forest, and people from the city raced to put it out. "The shortcut would've brought us into that fire."

"Let's see if we can help," Will said, leading the way.

Will, Leata, and Tivona spent the next several hours helping to minimize the spread of the deadly fire, but to no avail. The townspeople watched in horror as large trees creaked and swayed and began to topple.

Tivona watched one tree sway, unaware she stood in the path of another falling tree. Will, too far to help her, put his hand to his mouth to shout a warning.

Just then, a young man darted from the crowd, grabbed Tivona's arm, and pulled her from its lethal path. She landed on the ground, a stunned look on her face, and then turned toward the young man's outstretched hand. Tivona turned away from the man as if refusing his help, but then she seemed to notice him anew, as if his wavy brown hair, handsome blue eyes, and friendly smile had caught her off guard.

"I'm very sorry. Can I help you up, Miss?"

Tivona accepted his hand, and he lifted her to her feet. "Thank you. You just saved my life!"

Will and Leata strode toward them, overhearing their exchange.

"I'm not in the habit of tossing young women to the ground," he said, "but I'm glad you're safe. My name is Stephen."

She shook his hand. "I'm Tivona."

"That is a nice name. I haven't heard it before."

"We were on our way to Sumara. Oh, this is my sister, Leata, and this is Will."

"You couldn't have traveled through the forest with that fire," Stephen said.

"No, luckily, we had some wise advice not to go that way." Tivona glanced at Will. "Can you tell us how close we are?"

Stephen smiled. "I'm heading back to Sumara myself. Would you mind if I escorted you?"

"I'm sure she wouldn't," blurted Leata, but then Tivona stepped on her foot.

Turning to Will, Stephen asked, "Do you mind if I walk with you guys, Will?"

"Not at all," Will said.

Approaching a chestnut brown horse, Stephen took the reins and led the way down the dirt road toward the town.

Leata's eyes glowed as she marveled at the impressive animal and stroked its brow. "She is so beautiful. Is she yours?"

Nodding, a broad smile spread over Stephen's face. "Here, why don't you get on and ride alongside us."

Wasting no time, Leata stuck her foot in the stirrup and mounted smoothly as if no stranger to horses. She rubbed the groomed hair on its neck. "What's her name?"

"Lizzy." Stephen handed her the reins and then walked alongside Tivona and Will to Sumara.

Chapter 14

They entered the arched stone gates of Sumara, and Will turned himself in circles to marvel at the tall architecture of the grand buildings with ornate fluted columns. "This is something." The town seemed more advanced than Eppita as they moved past buildings with signs they were schools of science and medicine.

Stephen walked next to his chestnut horse. "We used to be part of a great nation, rich in more than material ways, but we lost something important. I feel as if something is coming to make us answer for our lack of sincerity and heart."

Tivona strode a few paces ahead of the others. "That sounds serious but not unlike my own home. What do you think is coming? And do you know when?"

Shrugging, Stephen replied, "I don't know the answer to either question. I don't know if it's a test of our perseverance, a trial of suffering, or an all-out war of good versus evil. I just know something is imminent." Then he shook his head. "I'm sorry to go on like that. Here I am welcoming you to my great home, and I sound like I am putting it down. Sumara has a great many good and honest people, but we need to come together to regain the richness we once had. The problem is that renewal might take sacrifices people aren't willing to make."

Tivona gazed at Stephen with admiration as he spoke, but when he turned his blue eyes her way, she quickly looked elsewhere.

"I didn't have a chance to ask, but what brings you to Sumara?" Stephen asked Will.

"I'm searching for my younger brother, Sam, and also my three friends who came on this journey to help find him."

"And you think they're in Sumara?"

"I don't know. I only knew that I needed to travel through Eppita and Sumara for some reason. I can't explain any more than that." Beyond the book's messaging, Will wished he knew more and felt hopeful again. But how many times could he gain hope only to have it dashed?

Stephen ran his hand through his hair. "I think I would've known if any young boys had traveled this way or were being held in Sumara against their will. That doesn't mean they couldn't be here, but it's unlikely. I know someone we can ask, though."

A small "Ahem" came from somewhere close to Will. Before Stephen could ask, a louder "Ahem!" came from the pouch, making Stephen scratch his head.

Will reached in and scooped Stitch up into the palm of his hand.

Stephen shook his head, smiling. "Who is this little guy?"

"This little guy is Stitch," Stitch said. "Tivona heard that another Kiggle might have been seen in your town. A young girl may be keeping them as toys, which we are not."

Stephen bowed his head humbly. "I didn't mean to insult you. I haven't seen any Kiggles, but I've heard about a family who might do such a thing." Stephen stopped in front of an entryway to the courtyard of a house. "This is my home, and I'd be honored if you'd come in to rest and have something to eat. Leata, can you walk Lizzy back to her stable?"

Leata bobbed her head, grinning, appearing more than happy to take care of her new friend.

Stephen let them in through the back door and led them to the kitchen area, where a woman chopped vegetables at a counter. "May, I've brought some hungry travelers from far away. Can we offer them anything as a welcome to our home?"

May glanced up at Stephen with a weary look. This likely wasn't the first time he'd surprised her with last-minute guests to feed. "I'm sure we can find something. Now, make sure those shoes aren't dirtying up my clean floor."

Stephen laughed and offered them a fruit bowl before cutting up a strawberry for Stitch. After biting into an apple, he yelled down the hallway, "Father, we have company!" Then he motioned for them to follow him down the hall past a series of rooms before they found his father working on a painting.

The older man had shoulder-length gray hair, wire-rimmed glasses on the end of his nose, and a once white smock now covered with an array of colors. He stood before a large canvas.

"Father, I brought some guests."

His father stopped mid-brushstroke and put down his paints to greet the strangers. He smiled at Tivona. "Stephen is always bringing home new people. Who do we have today?"

"This is Tivona."

They shook hands.

"I hope I didn't get any paint on you." Stephen's father wiped his hands on an old rag, then turned to Stephen. "She's got an impressive grip for such a beautiful woman. Good combination."

Tivona blushed, then shifted an admiring gaze toward Stephen as he introduced Leata, Will, and Stitch.

"This is my father, Joshua, the wisest and most loving person I know."

Joshua returned an awkward smile at the compliment, then he glanced at Tivona, who still gazed with admiration at Stephen.

May entered the room with a large tray of fruit, meats, bread, cheeses, and a large pitcher of iced lemon water.

Bowing to May, Joshua waved everyone toward a long table in the next room. "Sit. Sit. Let's eat and hear about your adventure."

"Thank you." Will shuffled to the table and pulled out a chair. "We are kind of hungry and tired from the trip. My brother's name is Sam. He disappeared along with my friends, and we're searching for them. We were guided to come this way."

"Interesting." Joshua toyed with a cluster of grapes and then looked up. "There must be some reason you were sent to Sumara. I sense that something significant is coming to this land—not just to Sumara but to the land of a once mighty kingdom. I don't mean mighty in the sense of conquering other nations but mighty in the sense of its internal strength, in each citizen as part of the whole.

"When people started putting themselves before others, we lost something important, and the whole began to break apart and become less. I think it's time for us to become whole again, and that will take courage, integrity, fortitude, and trust in the source of our strength. It will also take leadership, a new king with integrity, humility, and love for his people." Joshua nodded at his son and then peered directly into the eyes of each of his visitors. "I feel the time is near."

Stephen shook his head. "Father, Stitch believes one of

his family members might be held in Sumara. Do you have any idea what family might want to own such a little one as Stitch?"

Joshua's bushy gray eyebrows drew together as he gazed at Stitch and sighed. "I do, but I don't believe they would give their possession up easily."

Stitch stood taller. "Where are they? Can we go there?"

"They live in that large home on the east side, near the old school, but it could be dangerous. As far as Will's brother and friends go, I don't believe they are in Sumara any longer, but I believe the boy may have been here several days ago."

Will sat up straighter, gaining a glimmer of hope. "Do you know where he went?"

"I'm sorry, but I don't. Your best bet will be to proceed to Perggia. It's not an easy route nor one without danger. I hesitate even to suggest it, but I understand what family means. You will need help, though. The route will take you through a treacherous pass well-guarded by the Taker's vicious army. That liar stole the Perggian throne from a good king by deceit and tricks, turning the city against the Giver. Today, the struggle for the soul of the Perggian people comes to a boiling point, much like here."

Joshua's painting caught Will's attention, so he walked over for a closer look. "Are you trying to capture the struggle you talk about in this painting?"

Tivona joined Will by the painting. The left side depicted people with sheer terror on their faces, sinking into a collapsing pit, weighed down by the things they clutched onto. In contrast, people on the right, dressed in white garments, were elevated. A man wearing a king's crown mounted on a horse struggled to pull the sinking people out of the pit with ropes.

Coming between them, Joshua said, "You have a good eye, Will. Our souls can lift us to greatness, but hopelessly clutching onto things that don't matter leads to our death and destruction. We have lost trust in the good and what matters most."

Tivona turned to him, her brow furrowed in worry. "How do you know this?"

Joshua gazed sadly at the man on the horse in his painting. "Some things, you just know."

Chapter 15

"That's the house." Stephen pointed to a lavish white two-story home in a nice neighborhood on the east side of town. "I've heard stories about how this family made its fortune by means that weren't anything to be proud of. I'm not exactly sure what we will run into."

His brows rising, Stitch's eyes rounded.

"I guess we just have to take a chance. Ready, Stitch?"

With little hesitation, he nodded.

Standing hidden in a copse of trees, Will glanced down at his little friend, who had ridden in the pouch hanging from Will's shoulder. "I don't know, Stephen. What if Stitch gets caught? And the family tries to keep him, too?" Stephen had convinced the others that his plan would work and that it was the only way to find out if one of Stitch's family members lived here, but Will's protectiveness for his new friend made him reluctant to go along with it.

"Don't worry, Will." Stephen lifted Stitch from the pouch and held him at eye level. "Ready, Stitch?"

"Yes, sir." Stitch climbed into a pocket of Stephen's coat, huffing and grunting as he settled into it. "My, but it's a tight fit in here," he mumbled.

"Stay out of view," Stephen said to Will. Then he strode down a long driveway, heading for the big front door.

Will leaned against a thick tree trunk, watching them go, anxiety building. "I don't think I can just wait here." Hoping Stephen wouldn't turn around and catch him, he took off for the house, cut across the lawn, and dove behind a thick holly bush next to the front porch.

Stephen rapped the knocker on the large front door and cleared his throat. Within seconds, the door creaked open.

Not wanting Stephen or the resident to see him, Will peeked between the spiky leaves of the holly bush.

A larger-than-life manservant, resembling a bodyguard more than a butler, peered down at Stephen. "How may I help you?" he rumbled.

Without giving a reply, Stephen stepped over the manservant's boot and into the foyer.

Eyebrows lowering with a look of surprise, the manservant jerked back but then flung an arm out and stopped Stephen's advance. "You cannot barge in here."

Heart hammering in his chest, Will climbed onto the porch, pressed himself to the wall, and spied through the open door. He didn't want to get caught and risk blowing their plan, but he had to know if Stitch would be safe.

Stephen, playing his role, looked the tall man over, then pushed the eyeglasses he had borrowed from his father up higher on the bridge of his nose. "Forgive the intrusion, but this is an emergency. I am an inspector from the government offices, and there is a mandate to check every home in the area for fire hazards. I'm sure you heard about the raging forest fire. You don't want this whole town brought to ashes, do you?"

"No, sir." A flash of uncertainty gave way to a more rigid expression. "However, the lord and lady of the house are not home. Come back at another time if you must."

Stephen waved his hand, pulled out a notebook, and turned to the nearest window as if inspecting it. "There is no time to lose. This is an emergency edict, and I must do my job." He jotted down a note and then ascended the second-floor staircase.

"I must protest. You must leave now." The man huffed and puffed up the stairs after him.

As the manservant reached the top step, Will slipped through the open door. Once the servant rounded the corner, Will ascended the carpeted staircase and hid behind a large potted plant in the corner of the upstairs hallway.

"That doesn't look safe. And what's that?" Stephen's loud voice came from the room at the furthest end of the hallway. "I don't see any exits in case of fire."

"The exits are downstairs," the manservant said, an edge of anger in his tone. "And one can always climb out a window."

"Hmm. Too high," Stephen replied. "People could get hurt."

In the next moment, a little voice came from nearby. "Don't get caught!"

Will nearly jumped out of his skin. Had someone spotted him? He risked glimpsing around the plant. Then he exhaled and had to suppress a laugh.

With a sneaky smile on his face, Stitch stood in the middle of the hallway. Stephen must've put him down stealthily to allow him to search for other Kiggles. He waved at Will and then darted into the nearest room. A few seconds later, he popped out of the room and dashed into another. Stephen and the man continued discussing fire safety while Stitch sneaked from one room to another.

Will counted doors in the hallway and considered helping with the search. If he moved quietly, he didn't need to remain hidden behind the plant, did he? He could always check—

"What's up there?" Stephen shouted, pointing to the ceiling. He and the man had returned to the hallway.

Will flattened himself against the wall, praying no one

could see him behind the plant, even though he could still see them between the leaves. And wait—oh no!

Stitch was stuck under the door to a room near Will, his head poking into the hallway. He'd apparently started crawling out just as Stephen and the man had left the room on the opposite end of the hallway.

Stephen pointed to the ceiling. "Up there? What's up there?"

The man turned his face upward. "An attic, of course."

"Well, attics can be very dangerous, you know." Stephen's eyes shifted to Stitch.

Stitch, back on his feet now, gave him the thumbs-up sign and pointed to the door of the room he'd just left. It was the only one in the hallway with a glass knob. Was a Kiggle in there?

"Dangerous? Why would the attic be dangerous?" the man shouted. "Are you sure you work for the—"

"Wait," Stephen blurted, "are there any children's rooms on this floor?"

The man rolled his eyes. "Yes, down the hall. Why do you need to know this? What difference does it make whose room—"

"Well, certainly, we want to protect the young ones most. Come, come, show me the room."

The man stomped down the hallway toward the potted plant and Will and the door with the glass knob.

Holding his breath and fighting panic, Will shuffled between the planter and the wall, keeping the foliage between him and the man.

The man flung open the door to a room with soft colors and frilly bed pillows. He raised his hand and huffed. "Okay, you've seen it. Now, it is time for you to finish your inspection and leave."

While Stephen replied and jotted notes in his notebook and the man argued with him, Stitch took the opportunity to sneak back into the room. Half-hidden behind a red ball, Stitch made eye contact with Stephen, then pointed to a small wire cage on top of a desk under the window.

Taking notes and arguing with the man, Stephen entered the room and stumbled. His notebook fell at the man's feet, and his hand bumped the desk. Wait—did he just unlatch the cage? Before the man straightened up with the notebook, Stephen also managed to place Stitch behind a doll on the desk.

"Take your notebook and go," the man shouted, slapping it into Stephen's hand.

What was the rest of the plan? How could Stephen get both Stitch and the other Kiggle out of the room under the man's watchful eye?

"Okay, okay," Stephen said, leaning over the desk, "but first, I detect the odor of gas. Let me just open this—" He managed to open the window just before the man grabbed his arm and tugged him away from it.

Will took the opportunity to make his exit. He knew now how he could help. He rushed for the stairs and descended the steps with barely a sound. Then he raced through the front door, which hung open, and ran around to the side of the house under the girl's bedroom window.

Little Stitch and another Kiggle peered out of the window.

Will lifted his hands. "Jump, and I'll catch you!"

Stitch and the other Kiggle exchanged glances, then leaped together from the open window and safely into Will's arms.

"Oh, phew," someone said, coming around the corner of the house.

Not taking any chances, Will tucked the Kiggles into his pouch and turned.

A smiling Stephen stood behind him, tucking his father's glasses into his coat pocket. "How'd you know which room they were in?"

"Let's get away from the house." Will led the way back to the cluster of trees where Stephen had originally left him. Then he opened the pouch to bring the two Kiggles out, but Stitch held the other Kiggle in a tight hug, tears streaming down his green cheeks.

When they finally separated, Will lifted them out.

Holding the other Kiggle's hand, Stitch raised his gaze to Will and Stephen. "Thank you, both of you. This is my wife. Neive, meet Will and Stephen. I would never have found you without them. Do you know if the children are safe?"

She shook her head, her eyes filling with tears. "I worry for them. Many of us were kidnapped together and sold off to families as amusements. They were sold in another town. I don't know the name, but I think it is south of us."

Stitch squeezed her hand, a look of determination in his eyes. "We will find them. I promise you; I will not give up until they are safe."

Will crouched down. "Neive, it's an honor to meet you. You have a good husband. He's helped me in more ways than I can count. I'll do whatever I can to help find your family."

"And I," said Stephen.

Neive smiled in gratitude, and Will placed them carefully back into his pouch. "I'm going to have to find a pouch big enough for your whole family."

As the rescue team opened the courtyard door, Tivona and Leata dashed out of Stephen's house. Will brought the two Kiggles out and made the introductions.

"I'm so glad your mission was a success," Leata said, beaming with happiness.

"Pleased to meet you." Tivona shook Neive's little hand. "I'm so happy you were rescued."

"Me too," Will said. "But now we've got to get going. The family will likely come looking for her. So it's on with our original mission."

May packed enough food for several days while Stephen readied the horses.

Tivona gave Stephen a grateful smile. "We can't take your beautiful horses from you."

Stephen continued saddling the horses. "Who said you're taking them? I'm going with you, and I'll bring them safely back home."

"Why would you do that for us? We just met you," Tivona said, stroking the cream-colored horse named Abby.

Stephen laughed. "And you and your sister are old friends of Will's?"

She laughed. "I guess I can't argue that point."

Leata took a liking to the black horse called Winnie, while Tivona chose the pale horse named Abby, and Will made quick friends with the white horse called Reggie. Stephen's father, Joshua, gave his son a long hug and a blessing before letting him go. Finally, the group set off to Perggia.

Chapter 16

Will guided his horse around a deep rut in the rugged trail. Spiky plants and trees with gnarled trunks dotted the rough mountainous terrain around them. "I'm glad you let us borrow your horses, Stephen. I'd probably twist my ankle trying to navigate down this part of the trail."

Leata rode up between Will and Stephen and glanced at each with a broad smile on her face. Then she raced ahead of them; the black horse, Winnie, moved effortlessly over rocks and ruts.

As the trail narrowed, Will let his horse fall a few paces behind Tivona and Stephen, who rode side by side.

Tivona seemed to study Stephen for a moment. "Your father is quite proud of his son, but I think he loves him even more."

"He is a great man, and I admire him."

"And you love him too."

Stephen dipped his head and gave her a little smile. "And I love him too. I lost my mother when I was little, so we've been very close, and May has done her best to take care of us. I couldn't ask for more, but I often wonder what it would've been like if my mother was still with us—not just for me, but for Dad too."

A tear traced a path down Tivona's cheek, glistening in the sunlight. She turned away and wiped her face, the tilt of her head showing how Stephen's sincerity touched her. Maybe she even wondered what life would have been like if her father were alive. Leata once said Tivona had become skeptical of men after falling in love with a young man, only to have him disappear.

"I like that painting your father was working on," Will said, wanting to lighten the mood. "He has talent, and the movement of his brushstrokes is great."

Stephen glanced at Will over his shoulder, seeming relieved for the change of subject. "He does enjoy it. He's good at anything he puts his mind to."

"The man and horse in the painting looked an awful lot like you and Lizzie." Will nodded to indicate Stephen's reddish-brown mare.

Stephen laughed. "You think so? He is always asking me to pose for him, but I keep putting him off. He gets some crazy ideas sometimes."

"You mean like believing you are destined to wear the crown and bring this kingdom back together again in peace and greatness?" Tivona threw him a glance but then urged her horse forward, waiting for a response.

As they progressed further into the mountains, the trail became steeper and more difficult to navigate, even for the four young horses. At one point, it narrowed to a tight rock path notched out of the edge of a vertical cliff that wound around the mountain. Will nervously peered down at the stomach-churning drop. "Man, is that far down. I don't know how safe this is. What do you guys think?"

Leata peered down too. "Stephen's father said the only way to Perggia included a treacherous pass. This may be the only way."

Stephen scratched his head with a worried glance locked on the view below. "I don't know. This doesn't look good, but I think Leata is right about it being the only route. I'll go first since Lizzie is less likely to panic."

As they carefully rode along the narrow rock path, Will tried to keep his anxiety in check. He didn't normally think of himself as afraid of heights, but this drop was so far down that fear gripped his insides. No one spoke as their horses clomped along, and they listened for Stephen's warnings of unstable rocks. The jim-jams in Will's chest grew even stronger when they reached the halfway point. There was no turning back. And the view of the gorge below revealed their path had become even steeper. One false step, and they would fall to their deaths.

Suddenly, the cliff beneath Lizzie's hind legs gave way. "Hi-ya!" Stephen shouted, urging his horse forward. Lizzie pounded the trail with her front hoofs while her hind legs attempted to grip the rocks that were giving way.

Will forced himself past the fright and commanded his horse to stop.

Leata let out a panicked scream. Tivona gasped. They could only watch what looked like a certain fall into the deadly chasm below.

At last, Lizzie regained her footing and carried Stephen to safe ground. Everyone sighed in relief.

"Good girl, Lizzie!" Leata shouted across the broken path.

"Are you all right?" Tivona yelled.

Stephen placed his forefinger on his lips and whispered, "Shhh. We're okay, but I don't want to cause an avalanche." He inspected the ten-foot opening in the path where the rocks had given way.

"What are we going to do?" Tivona gripped her horse's reins.

Will turned to Leata and Tivona. "I think you two will need to go back."

"And what are you going to do, Mr. Will, fly over?" Leata

asked with a dubious expression.

Suspecting what he had to do, Will sighed and eased the leather book from the pouch. He opened the map. Their trail led straight ahead. "This is the only passageway. I need to make this jump."

"You're going to try to leap across *that*?" Leata's tone went from joking to concern as she peered down into the chasm.

"I have to, but I want you both to go back." Will stuffed the book into the pouch, careful not to bump his little friends.

"We're sticking with you," Stitch said, clinging to Neive as the two of them hunkered down in the pouch.

"If you can make that jump, Will, we certainly can," Tivona said.

Stephen motioned to them. "I know the horses can do it, but you need to back it up and make sure you land on this narrow spot."

They dismounted and backed the horses down the path. Then Will mounted his white horse, took several deep breaths, and patted the horse's side.

Stephen kept his sights directly on Reggie. "You can do this, girl. Will, no hesitation on the jump."

"Okay, let's go." Adrenaline pumping through him, Will shouted, "Hi-ya!" and leaned forward, kicking the horse's sides, commanding it into action. Reggie galloped along and leaped—

Will and his white horse sailed through the air and landed, hooves scraping on loose gravel, clearing the opening with inches to spare. Relief flooding through him, Will exhaled and moved out of the way so the next could go.

Leata went next and sported a huge smile as she landed

safely across.

Going last, Tivona leaned forward with a look of concentration, then the horse took off and, with one great leap, cleared the dangerous section of the path and landed safely on the other side. Her relief quickly turned into alarm as the rocks under the horse's hind legs gave out, and she started to slip towards the steep drop.

In case of emergency, Will had been gripping the goblet in his pouch, but Stephen grabbed the horse's reins and pulled her forward with all his strength, bringing Tivona safely onto solid ground.

Leata dismounted and approached Tivona on her horse when a boulder from above slammed down next to her, quickly followed by another.

"Avalanche!" Stephen shouted.

Everyone mounted their horses and took off along the narrow path, dodging more falling rocks until they cleared the narrow path on the cliff. Will followed Stephen as the trail wound higher up the mountainside. As they rounded a bend, people came into view—families heading toward them.

"Hello there! How is everyone this fine day? It looks like you were able to make your way across the cliff," bellowed one of the men with a broad smile.

Stephen pointed back toward the trail. "We ran into some trouble with a rock slide. It wouldn't be safe for anyone to cross now."

The man took off his worn hat and scratched his head. "It's never an easy hike, but it's our only way back."

Will dismounted and stepped forward. "Impossible. Besides the falling rocks, a section of the path has collapsed. You'll have to find another way."

An older woman approached Will. She wore a kerchief

over her hair and an old rough cloth over her shoulders. "We appreciate your thoughtful concern," she said, revealing a few missing teeth as she spoke. "You look like a kind young man. Maybe you could help us?"

Will scratched his head. "I'm not sure what I can do. I'll help if I can." It was her he felt most worried about trying to cross the dangerous cliff path, even if they could manage the area that had given way.

She waved Will closer and whispered her request into his ear.

Will listened to her strained voice, trying to understand her words.

"I did not want to frighten your friends, but the path ahead is even more dangerous than the way you came. Please trust me to turn around and take the easy path instead."

Confused at how the path could be any more dangerous than what they had just narrowly survived, he replied, "I have to go on. I cannot leave my brother." Then he furrowed his brow as she peered up into his eyes, drawing him in.

She beckoned him with her crooked finger as her eyes narrowed. "Trust me. You and your friends will be safer to turn back and surrender your foolish quest. Bow to me instead of your pride, and you will be safe with us. "

He thought, *No!* Rising above the false security she offered, he made a move to draw his sword.

She gripped his shoulder harder, preventing him from action.

"Don't trust them!" he pointed at the newcomers. Regardless of the danger he would face, he would not give in.

The old woman jerked back, her eyes popping open

wide, making her look almost as surprised as Stephen.

"Will, what are you doing?" Stephen said.

Tivona gasped, then screamed, "Watch out!"

The woman began to increase in size, and hair sprouted on her body. She changed into a beastly-looking creature, as did the other travelers.

Leata galloped forward and swung her sword, causing the creature to release its grip on Will. Stephen drew his sword as another creature threatened to pull him from his horse. Before he could strike, Tivona reared back with her bow and loosed an arrow with force, sending the attacking creature to its knees.

A dozen more creatures scuttled toward them, coming from around the bend in the trail. As the next beast hurled his large hairy body at them, Will caught it with a lunge of his sword. Leata smiled with relief before turning her attention to another attacker.

"These are Jacobines," yelled Will. He doubted that they could handle them. "There are so many of them."

"Don't give up, Will." Stephen hit one creature over the head, then pierced another, who made a whaling sound.

A beast pulled Leata off her mount. As she landed flat on her back, the creature drew his sharp claws back, preparing to strike, but then an arrow pierced him through his chest. Leata turned toward Tivona, who gave a single nod before turning with her bow to another threat.

Stephen fought off two more while Will instinctively threw his sword like a javelin into the fierce-looking creature approaching the group from behind. As the number of attackers decreased, Will's spirits lifted. The good guys were going to win!

But even as hope stirred him onward, a swirling ball of

black mist appeared in the fray . . . and the beasts backed away in fear.

Will caught his breath as the disturbing black mist slithered around itself in the air before him. "Will—*s-s-s-s*. While you may be brave and s-s-s-stronger than when we last met, you are no match for me. I could s-s-s-send a thousand more of these warriors-*s-s-s-s* and you wouldn't stand a chance, so you should be grateful for my s-s-s-spoiling you."

Shaking inside, Will tried not to show fear. "I will never bow to you."

A gloating laugh came from the mist. "Not even to s-s-s-save your own brother? Or your friends-s-s-s? Or these young ladies-s-s-s?" With that, the mist dissipated and disappeared, along with all the Jacobine soldiers, but the eerie laugh continued in the distance, echoing throughout the gorge.

Chapter 17

Will glanced quickly around. Open-mouthed, Leata asked, "What was that about?"

Will shrugged. "I wish I knew. It's been haunting me from the beginning of this journey to find my brother."

"I can't imagine it's anything good." Tivona cleaned an arrow from the ground and dropped it into her quiver.

Stephen squeezed Will's shoulder. "There's got to be a good reason for his interest in you. My father believes the time is near for people to choose their side."

"Why would that have anything to do with me?" Will said.

"I don't know. We probably all have a role, but leaders are chosen from the most unexpected places. The evil one won't give up until he wins, so—" Stephen let his sentence hang.

"So?" Tivona dropped another arrow into her quiver and straightened.

"So, we'd better get moving. I don't trust this place." Stephen mounted his horse, and Tivona watched him with curious interest. They rode for several more hours until the sun began to set, and then they stopped on a hill overlooking a magnificent valley. "This might be a good place to camp for the night. What does everyone think?"

Everyone agreed, so they settled their horses and then sat together to marvel at the changing colors of the brilliant sunset. After a long moment of silence, Tivona tapped Stephen's leg. "So, what exactly does your father think will happen?"

"Well, he talks about the kingdom that once existed in

harmony with our belief in the Giver, and what was good for the whole united us. Gradually, people stopped trusting and became more interested in their own plans and interests. Bickering and disagreements became violent, and even battles erupted, separating us more. Then, the storm winds, droughts, and plagues made the fertile lands a barren desert and wilderness. People were suffering, and they believed in the empty promises of the Taker to save them." Stephen turned away from the sunset and made eye contact with Will. "He's a very convincing liar. My father thinks the time is coming for everyone to choose an allegiance to the good or the evil, and the only way to defeat the forces of the Taker is to do it together as one united kingdom."

"And he thinks that will require a leader?" Tivona said. "A new king to unite the towns and cities—am I guessing right?"

Stephen nodded.

"And he knows who that king will be?" she said.

Stephen shook his head. "No. No one can know. Not even that person himself knows. He is to be chosen from an unexpected source."

The evening darkness came quickly, and the campfire glowed warmly on each of their faces. Will gazed into the distant night sky lit by the stars, then pointed southeast. "What's in that direction?"

Stephen turned. "That's where we just came from, Sumara. Why do you ask?"

Will peered up at the night sky. "That bright star just above it. I've seen a similar star over three other places: Lydia, Eppita, and Sumara, but not any other place."

"I would like to say that it's following you, but it's been straight above my hometown for as long as I can remember." Stephen pointed toward the northwest sky. "There's one there over Perggia."

"Hmm. It doesn't seem as bright as the ones over the other cities, though. How many cities are in the kingdom?" Will asked.

"Let's see, umm—there are seven. It would seem like whoever becomes king would have to have been to all seven." Stephen poked the wood in the fire with a long stick. "I do know that we've got a long day tomorrow. I'll keep watch first if you guys want to get some sleep."

Leata stood and paced around the fire. "I can't relax after what happened today. How do we know this is a safe spot and that they aren't waiting for us to let down our guard?"

Will wondered the same thing. He pulled out his leather book and opened it and there was no more writing than what he had seen before. Remembering the guidance to trust, he laid his head on a grassy spot and gazed up at the multitude of stars above. The uncountable lights in the sky seemed to go on forever.

Sam came to Will's mind. His little brother had irritated him at times, not leaving Will alone when he wanted to be alone, but Will missed him. He missed his uncountable questions, which might have challenged even the stars in the sky. Why had he found Sam so annoying all the time? Sam didn't have a father either, but he did have an older brother. Will regretted his cold behavior toward Sam. Maybe he'd been jealous of his little brother—or just selfish. Regret tumbled around in Will's mind as he drifted off to sleep.

Early in the morning, Will's body jolted. Something had kicked his leg. He tightened his grip on the hilt of his sword, which he always kept at the ready.

"Time to get up." Leata stood over him, smiling. Not some treacherous beast ready to tear him apart.

"Don't do that!" Will released his grip on the sword and sat up.

"I'm not the one with a sharp sword in my hand!" Leata said.

Will had the feeling she'd been watching him sleep until she got bored. "I'll remember that next time you try to give someone a heart attack."

"I've been keeping guard for the past few hours after his watch." She nudged Stephen's shin, and he jerked awake. She smiled.

After a light breakfast, they started their day's journey to Perggia. The ride down the hill into the valley was beautiful and peaceful, especially compared to the previous day's events. Stephen kept peering back at the trail behind them.

Will caught up. "Stephen, are you worried someone is following us?"

He glanced back again. "I don't know. I'm probably being paranoid, but I have an uneasy feeling. That voice in the black mist spooked me, although he seems focused on you in particular."

"I can't figure out why. I'm no threat to him. I'm just looking for my brother and friends," said Will.

"There must be some reason," said Tivona from behind.

For the rest of the ride, Will struggled to answer that question but came up empty. They finally reached Perggia. The city's history was carved into its elaborate gates. The bustling town inside the gates resembled Sumara, but with a different feel. People seemed less friendly, more preoccupied as they scurried to their destinations, often bumping into Will and the others without apologizing.

Stephen waved the group to the right. "I know someone who might care for the horses and put us up for the night." He scanned the crowd through narrowed eyes as if searching for suspicious characters.

They slowed in front of a home with a similar courtyard but more modest than Stephen and his father's home. They led the horses into the courtyard, where an old man cranked a hand pump, filling a bucket with water. "Stablehand, would you have any water for a thirsty horse named Lizzie?" Stephen shouted.

The man spun to face him, a beaming smile on his face. "Steph! Steph, my lad, how I've missed you so."

Without hesitation, Stephen rushed over and embraced the man. "Solly. It is so good to see you too. It's been too long, but my father hasn't been able to travel this way."

The man shifted his gaze to Will, Tivona, and Leata. "And you brought friends with you, Steph."

"Yes. This is Tivona and her sister, Leata. And this young man is Will."

"Honored to meet you. My name is Solomon."

"I couldn't pronounce it when I was little, so 'Solly' was easier," Stephen said.

Inside, Solomon provided his visitors with a place to wash and food to eat. As they sat at the kitchen table, he asked, "So, what is the purpose of your travel?"

Will took a sip from his drink and sat back. "We are trying to find my brother, Sam, and three of my friends who are lost—and two children of a friend of mine. Even though we just met, Stephen, Tivona, and Leata have generously offered to help me."

Solomon nodded, looking around the table. "I'm impressed by your courage and willingness to help others in need. Times are dangerous around these parts. How small are the two children?"

Will glanced at his fellow travelers. "Very small." As he answered, his pouch shifted and drew Solly's gaze.

Solly laughed and pointed to the pouch. "I assume you mean that literally?"

Stitch wiggled his way out of the pouch. "Size is relative and doesn't make you less!" Neive appeared beside him.

"Was Will referring to your children?" Solomon leaned closer to the tiny couple. They quietly nodded. "I may be able to help you."

Their expressions became jubilant. "How can you help us?"

"I'm aware of the plight of Kiggles, how they've been kidnapped and taken into slavery as entertainment or playthings. It's not right. I may know of a household keeping two Kiggles. I don't know if they are your children, but it's worth finding out."

Neive put her hand to her mouth, her eyes filling with tears. "Thank you so much."

Solomon turned to Will. "I may also be able to help you."

Will raised his head with intense interest. "How?"

"Well, I saw an outfit like yours several days ago on a young man. I thought it was unique until I saw you. Now I'm wondering if it could be someone you know."

"It has to be Porty or Arrie! Where is he? Can we go now?"

Solomon grabbed Will's shoulder. "Well, that's the tough part. He is at the palace, and I think he is being held there against his will."

Chapter 18

Will's stomach filled with butterflies as he and Solomon approached the granite steps of the palace in the center of Perggia. Guards flanked the main gate and stood on various levels of the stairs of this massive building with majestic columns and two twelve-foot-tall wooden doors.

Guards barred the entrance, asking Will and his mates questions. No one questioned or tried to stop Solomon, a respected elder in town, but only gave him respectful nods. An ornate hall came off the entryway, with people attending to what looked like important business. No one seemed to notice them as they walked the white marble halls.

Solomon pointed to the staircase. "The grand marble staircase leads to the centuries-old king's throne room. A leader of the town, who does not have the official title of king, occupies the throne now and, in effect, rules. I like him. He is an amicable and charismatic leader. He has the people's confidence."

"Does this place have a dungeon?" Leata said, eyes wide.

"Yes." Solomon's eyes twitched. "Prisoners are kept somewhere below the palace, but I don't know how to get to it."

As Solomon and the others agreed to watch for signs of guards coming from the prisons below, Will climbed the marble steps to the top, where six men stood guard at two heavy-looking golden doors. Will peered down the ornate hallways for another entrance, but then he spotted someone wearing a musketeer outfit!

Not trusting his eyes, he rubbed them. But when he opened them again, there he was: Porty. Will waved, and Porty ran to him.

"Will!" Porty pulled him into a quick hug. "We thought we lost you forever! Are you okay?"

"Yeah. Are *you* okay? We? Is everyone else here? Did you find Sam?"

"Let's see. Yes. No. Yes." Porty tapped his chin.

"Wait a minute. Yes, no, yes?"

"Yes, I'm okay. No, everyone else is not here. Yes, I found Sam. And that's not all." Porty cracked a smile.

Even more confused, Will shook his head. "Wait, wait, wait. You're okay. Is it safe being here?"

"Sure. I'm being well taken care of. You should see the food they have!"

"But you said you found Sam. Where is he? Arrie and Jules aren't here? Where are they?"

Porty shuffled one foot along the carpeted floor. "When we got separated from you, we were completely lost. After days of walking without any idea where we were going, an old beggar with a rickety cart and horse offered us a ride. He brought us here, giving us a place to stay and food to eat. The next day, those golden doors were open, and the king, or whatever he's called, was sitting on his throne talking to a young boy. I thought that moppy head looked familiar, and when he turned toward us, we realized it was Sam! We yelled Sam's name, and the man on the throne waved us in."

"So, what happened? Where's Sam now?" Will nearly burst with anticipation.

"I'm getting to that. Sam was safe here at the palace. He said he had been wandering for days before a man helped him get to Perggia. He rode on some kind of bird or something; I don't know. He was brought to the palace and was well taken care of. He told the man his story, and that is when Sam found out."

"Found out what, Porty? You're talking in riddles."

"He found out who the man on the throne was." Porty took a bite from a candy bar.

"Who? Who was he?"

Porty stared at Will for a moment. "He's your dad, Will. Isn't that great news? Sam found your dad right here."

Stunned, Will shook his head in disbelief. "What? Porty, how does he know it's our dad?"

"When Sam told him about the attic and the goblet, your dad knew he was Sam. Sam then realized the man on the king's throne was the same man in the photos he had been looking at his whole life at your home—and he's the real thing!"

"How do we know it's really him?" Will rocked back and forth on his boots. *Could it be true?* "What's his name?"

Porty led Will back down the marble stairs and into the grand foyer. He walked him to a high wall on the right and pointed at a large portrait. "His name is William. It's your dad, Will."

Will hesitated and then gazed up at the portrait, and there he was, that genuine smile and comfortable eyes like Will's grandfather's. He'd studied those photos of his father daily, praying he would return, so there was no mistaking that it was him.

"He is really a neat guy. He took care of us and sent out search parties to find you. He wanted to hear everything about you and what you were like now that you're thirteen."

"I can't believe it. Where is he? Where's Sam? What

happened to Jules and Arrie?" Hope, joy, and confusion battled inside Will as he gazed at the portrait of his father.

Porty's smile faded. "Jules and Arrie disappeared. There's evidence that they were kidnapped and taken out of the city. Your father pulled together many of his soldiers and went out to search for them. He asked me to stay here in case they returned or you came this way. Once he finds you, he doesn't want to lose you again."

Will paced the hallway, trying to decide what to do next. "So, where's Sam, then?"

"Sam pleaded with your father to go with him. Your father tried to convince him to stay here but finally gave in. They headed to Thytira, the city south of here."

Will spotted Solomon and the others and waved them over. "This is Porty, one of my friends I've been searching for." He turned to Porty. "And this is Solomon, the man who helped us find you. This is Leata, Tivona, and Stephen. Oh, and—" Will scooped Stitch and Neive into his hand. "We rescued Neive, Stitch's wife, but we need to find their two children. Solomon thinks they may be in Perggia. Porty just told me that he found my brother and father."

"Hi, Porty." Leata offered her hand. "Will, you didn't tell us you were looking for your father too."

"I didn't know I was. He disappeared ten years ago, leaving my mother and us alone. I thought he deserted us, but he must have come through that wall in the attic like we did."

"What attic? What wall? You're not making any sense, Will," Leata said.

"It's not important, but we mustn't lose time going after them."

Stephen nodded. “Solly and I already know each other. And we must try to rescue Stitch and Neive’s children if they are in Perggia. Solly, you said that you might be able to help find the house with the Kiggles to see if they are who we are looking for.”

Solomon nodded. “We’ll have to get the horses since their house is on the other side of the city.” He paused. “I will have to warn you that this family is involved with some sinister stuff. We’ll have to be careful.”

Chapter 19

They pulled up with their horses a few houses down from the large mansion where Solomon believed the Kiggles were being kept. Solomon said, “We can’t just walk in and ask these people for their Kiggles. This family didn’t get rich by thinking of others. Far from it. I’ll try to keep them occupied at the front door while you enter through the back.”

Will stopped at the corner of the house and turned back, shocked at what he saw.

Solomon took out a knife, cut his palm, and rubbed the crimson blood on the side of his head. He banged hard on the front door until the door opened, then he crouched as if in pain. Several servants rushed from the house to his aide.

In the meantime, the rest of the group slinked around the back and encountered one of the security guards. Leata used her secret grip and knocked him out. Stephen and Will dragged the unconscious man behind the shed. They entered through the back door and began searching the house.

After some searching, Will opened the last door on the third floor and found two Kiggles in a dollhouse enclosed with a gold-colored screen. As he worked to remove the screen, he let out Stitch and Neive. “Tara! Nino!” Neive said in a muffled voice and with tears in her eyes. “Hold on. We’re here to get you out.”

“Mama! Papa! They think we’re playtoys,” said Tara.

“Shhh.” Stitch pressed his forefinger against his pursed lips.

Finally, Will undid the fasteners just as Leata reached the room. Will let Stitch and Neive climb onto his palm. Tara and Nino walked from the little dollhouse onto his hand, too. With a flood of tears, Neive hugged Tara, and Stitch hugged Nino. Will lowered them into the pouch and secured the screen back in place.

Everyone smiled and gave an enthusiastic two thumbs up out in the hall. They quietly descended the back stairs, and Stephen signaled Solomon, who was still receiving care from the servants. Thankfully, none of the family was home.

"I'll be okay now," Solomon said, pushing helpful hands away from his head as he got to his feet. "Thanks for your kindness. I really need to get home."

Will raced out the back door but as he turned the corner and looked back, he jerked to a full stop.

Just as Solomon exited through the front door, a large, lavishly dressed man stepped onto the porch.

"I know you," the man bellowed. "Why are you here?"

Will and the others peeked around the corner. Unfortunately, the large man turned their way at the same moment.

"What's going on here?" the man shouted.

"Nothing," said Solomon, waving his hands as if to calm the man. "I had the wrong address."

One of the servants came to the front door. "Sorry, sir. He came to the front door bleeding, and we let him in."

"Stop them!" The security guard staggered from around the back of the house. "They took something. I'm sure of it."

Will and Solomon exchanged glances. The panic on Solomon's face reflected the dread inside Will. They needed to get away fast.

At that moment, four men arrived on horseback. The largest of them looked familiar—he was the manservant from the house in Sumara, where Will and Stitch rescued Neive. Pointing at Stephen, he shouted to the wealthy homeowner. "That's the man we told you about! The one we've been tracking from Sumara."

The manservant's master puffed up with anger. "No one takes anything from me, not even a Kiggle. Stop them!"

Not wanting the Kiggles to get hurt, Will shielded the pouch with his arm, and his eyes darted around for an escape route.

Solomon tried to push the homeowner aside, but the large man shoved him back, sending Solomon to the ground.

Stephen ran to help, but the even larger manservant leaped from his horse toward Stephen. He reared back with a clenched fist to give Stephen a blow in the head.

Will raced toward them and grabbed his arm, hoping to hold back his fist, but the manservant flicked him to the ground.

The other men dismounted and joined as Tivona, Leata, and Porty came onto the scene. Fighting ensued. Bodies flew, and it seemed certain Will's friends were outmatched.

As Will tumbled out of a servant's reach, he stuffed his hand into the pouch—wanting to check on the Kiggles—and his fingers brushed the metal of the goblet. The words were out before he realized what he'd said. "I wish we had help against these foes."

In an instant, a young man showed up with a glint in his eye and winked at Will. "Is this a private fight, or can anyone get in on it?"

The athletic young man pushed his wavy auburn hair from his brow, jumped the fence, and shoved back the large manservant about to stomp on Stephen's chest. The manservant turned, and the young man walloped him under the chin, sending him into the picket fence, toppling it. He put out his hand to help Stephen up. "Hi, I'm Jess. I do a little boxing on the side."

Next, Stephen and Jess freed Solomon and the girls from their entanglements, but there was no let up from these men who sported arrogant sneers of entitlement.

Solomon grabbed a ten-foot section of toppled picket fence in front of him, lifted it over his head, and slammed it down on six of the fighters while Jess held off the other two. "Steph, get the others out of here and take off on the horse!"

"Solly, I can't leave you!"

"Stephen, do as I say. Those mates of yours will need you." Wrestling to keep a servant from grabbing his neck, he turned to give Stephen a penetrating stare. "And, if your father is right, this kingdom will need you too. Get going. I can't hold them down forever."

Stephen walked backward for a few steps, his expression showing him torn between obeying and jumping back in the fight, then he turned and led the others to the horses. They took off as quickly as possible and rode out of town, heading for Thytira.

Chapter 20

Miles from Perggia, they stopped their frantic pace and let their horses rest. Will collapsed onto the ground and then opened the pouch to let Stitch and his family out. "I hope it's not too cramped in there?"

Stitch took the hand of a younger Kiggle. "Don't worry about that. I have my family back. We didn't have time earlier, but I want you all to meet Tara and Nino, my two beautiful children I've missed for far too long."

Will smiled. Stitch probably looked like Nino when he was a boy.

Nino pulled on his father's tunic. "Papa, there are more."

"There are more?" Stitch looked down at his son. "More what?"

"More of us. More Kiggles."

"We've seen hundreds rounded up and sold by the family," Tara said. "I think they took them out of town on this road."

"Looks like our visit to Thytira could become interesting. But I'm not sure a ragtag group like ours could handle a major fight," said Stephen.

Will grabbed Stephen's arm. "You knew we were being followed between Sumara and Perggia, didn't you?"

Stephen replied, "I had a funny feeling. It looks like it was our friends who were holding Neive."

"Do you think they will give up now?"

"Nope." No sooner had Stephen answered when footfalls pounded down the trail behind them.

Will jumped up in panic and drew his sword. Stephen

drew his sword, too, and both turned to see who approached while the others looked fearful.

In the next moment, two men were upon them, and Stephen sighed in relief. “What the heck are you doing here?”

Solomon smiled. “We missed you too, Steph. Did you think we were going to abandon you? I’m a hunted man now, as is our new friend, Jess.”

Will offered his hand. “Thank you, Jess, for helping us. It wasn’t looking too good before you arrived.” Will was well aware that he had used up another wish to get that help.

Jess shook Will’s hand. “Glad to be of assistance. The funny thing was that I was heading the other way but suddenly found myself near your fight. I’ll never figure out how that happened, but I couldn’t resist joining in a good fight like that.” Jess, who always seemed to have a smile on his face, punched his hand and then swung his arms to his sides. "So what's our mission in Thytira?"

“We’re searching for my brother, Sam, and friends, Arrie and Jules. Porty here tells me that my father, whom I haven’t seen since I was three, is with them too. I’m still having a hard time believing he’s actually here. Tara also tells us that hundreds of Kiggles are being held in Thytira.”

“Sounds like a good enough reason to join your band, if you don’t mind,” said Jess. “Either way, I’m from Thytira, so I’m heading your way.”

No one argued his offer.

“We welcome you.” Will tried guessing his age. Sixteen? Seventeen? His confident personality made him seem older. “It’ll be nice having someone with us who knows the next city and can fight so well.”

As the group walked along, questions rattled around Will's mind. Would he find Jules and Arrie? Would he finally rescue Sam? What weighed most on his mind was how he would feel about seeing his father. He couldn't remember a time when he didn't miss him or wonder what he was like and why he left them. They were a good family. Why would he desert them? Were they not good enough for him? Maybe it wasn't his father's fault. Maybe he couldn't get back home without the goblet.

After hours of travel and listening to Porty go on about his experiences, they stopped to camp for the night, still another half-day's journey before they would reach Thytira. They lit a fire, and everyone sat around telling stories as Will's mind drifted off, pondering his questions. The sky was full of stars again.

"I see two of those bright stars tonight." Will pointed to the one on his right and then the one on his left.

Solomon said, "Ahhh, the star. One always hangs over Perggia, and it looks like that one is over Thytira. Is that right, Jess?"

Jess gazed up into the sky. "I've gotten so used to seeing it there that I almost don't notice it anymore. You're right; that's Thytira. Do you think it means something?"

Stephen replied, "Maybe. Will said he has seen a similarly bright star over each city he has been to: Lydia, Eppita, Sumara, Perggia, and now Thytira. Five of the seven cities that made up the once unified kingdom."

"Hmm. I wonder if the stars are trying to tell us something important," said Jess.

Chapter 21

After several hours of riding in the morning, they reached the city of Thytira. Will marveled at the architecture that seemed more ancient than the other cities, with its fluted columns that held up massive stone buildings.

Riding his horse at a leisurely pace, Jess pointed out the grand hotels, stately homes, and government buildings until they reached one that looked like a palace.

Leata teased, “Jess, you’re not going to tell us you live here, are you?”

"Oh, well —" Jess dipped his head and gazed up at her, his cheeks turning pink. "Yeah, actually, this is home." Just then, the front gates opened.

A manservant took the reins of Jess’s horse as he dismounted. “Good to have you home safely, sir.”

Jess patted the man on the back. “Malcolm, it’s good to be back. We’ll be having guests tonight.”

“Very good.” Malcolm proceeded to assist Tivona and Leata with their horses, leading the group to the stables.

“Are you a prince or something?” Leata laughed.

Malcolm cleared his throat. “He won’t allow me to address him properly as Your Royal Highness.”

Leata’s eyes widened as she turned to Jess. “*Are* you?”

Jess chuckled. “Prince Jess doesn’t exactly roll off the tongue. I don’t like all the fanfare, but my mother is the queen of Thytira, and my late father was the king.”

Leata’s jaw dropped, and then she made an awkward attempt at a curtsy.

“We don’t need any of that, but if you’re going to do it,

you should do it right." Jess demonstrated a proper curtsy for a lady to make when she meets the queen. Leata giggled at the sight.

Will gazed upward at the ceilings high above, painted with scenes of the city and battles fought. The overwhelming beauty of the palace struck him as Leata pointed to various statues and paintings.

Suddenly, they froze as they entered a large room with gold-leaf walls and fancy adornments. A beautiful woman sitting on a throne turned and smiled at Jess. "Jess, who are your friends?"

Jess introduced his mother, the queen, and Leata tried her best to make a proper curtsy.

"Come, my dear. No formalities are necessary for friends of Jess. Where have you all come from?"

They approached and stood together, each in turn telling her their stories and their quest.

She responded, "You sense that something is about to happen, and I fear that it's true. There have been signs: the drought, locust attacks in our fields, and dying fish in the rivers. People will need to choose whom they want to follow, and a king will be chosen to lead a battle against the enemy."

Solomon nodded. "I have seen the signs myself, and I think you are right that a leader will emerge to fight and bring the scattered kingdom together." Solomon eyed Stephen, and the queen glanced towards her son, Jess . . . just as Will caught Stephen looking at him. All the while, Porty was busy tasting the variety of chocolates next to him, paying no attention to the serious conversation going on.

"Your Highness," Will said to the queen, "what would be the best way to find out if my brother, father, and friends are somewhere in Thytira?"

The queen turned to Jess. "Jess, can you send out several units of soldiers to find out if any of Will's family and friends have been seen in the city?"

Will lifted Stitch and his family out of the pouch. "And also any Kiggles. We have reports of hundreds who may be held captive and headed this way."

The queen glided over from her throne and lowered her head to look closer. "Did you say Kiggle?"

Stitch, Neive, Tara, and Nino all bowed. Stitch said, "That is correct. We are Kiggles, and thieves are kidnapping and selling us to families as playthings."

The queen shook her head. "No, no, no. That will never do. If we have any of your friends in our city, we will find them as well."

Stitch smiled.

A few minutes passed in quiet concentration, and then Jess strode back in with a group of armed soldiers in his wake. He pointed in the direction of the Kiggles, and his soldiers nodded. Then Jess stood, hands on hips, and faced Will and his friends. "Okay, let's get the search started." He motioned to his soldiers, who departed, then directed Will and the rest of the group to form search parties. Next, he led the way out of the palace and into the city streets.

Will and Leata paired up. After knocking at a dozen doors and questioning everyone they came across, Leata sighed as she walked beside him. "How are you feeling, Will?"

"About what?" Will turned to scan the steps of the library.

"About everything, like being so close to finding your brother and meeting your father after all this time?"

"I don't really know what I feel. Everything's been a whirlwind. I want to find Sam more than anything. My father? I've been dreaming about having a father ever since I can remember, but I don't know him. I feel a lot of things: curious, angry, scared. Part of me doesn't want to find him. Isn't that weird?"

Leata remained silent for several moments. "I would do anything to have my dad back again. I understand being scared and confused, but I think anything would be worth seeing him. You'll feel differently when you actually find him."

Several hours later, they returned to Jess's home to hear if the soldiers had uncovered any information. A man was seen with a young boy who may have fit Sam's description, but no one saw signs of Arrie, Jules, or Kiggles. The queen asked the head lieutenant to describe the man, and he seemed to fit the image in the painting in Perggia. "How did this man carry himself? Did he seem like he could be a king?"

The lieutenant rubbed his chin. "Something about him did draw one's attention. It's odd to think a king would come to your city without notice or greeting and in plain, humble clothes, but there was an air about him. When we tried approaching the man and the boy, we lost them in the crowd and couldn't find him again." As he finished, a soldier approached and whispered in his ear. Then, the lieutenant added to his report. "It appears that the man and boy were seen heading out of town toward Sidar. Would your Royal Highness like us to pursue him?"

The queen glanced at Jess and Will. "If he is a king, we have no right to bring him back, but would you like my soldiers to track him down for you?"

Will thought for a moment and then pulled out his

leather book, opening it to the next page. Writing appeared. *This is your quest; only you have been chosen to answer the call. Your courage and perseverance will make the difference.* Then, a path appeared on the page, winding its way from Thytira to Sidar. "Thank you for offering, but this is something I need to do myself." He turned to his fellow travelers. "Solomon, Stephen, Jess, Tivona, and Leata, I can't thank you enough for your courageous and selfless help getting me this far. I can't ask you to risk your lives any further."

After a long, somber silence, Leata said, "You don't know us very well if you think you can get rid of us that easily. Everyone can speak for themselves, but I'm not stopping now. No friend of mine is doing this alone. My own father would've stuck with you to the end, and I am my father's daughter."

Will was struck by Leata's words, her description of her father as a friend, and the type of loyalty their relationship was built on. His eyes teared up as he thought of his own family and friends. He'd had lapses in courage during this journey, but her response convicted him. He wanted to be as courageous and loyal to them as Leata was to him. Will said to Tivona, "I'm guessing that there's no way to change the mind of a stubborn sister, is there?"

Tivona smiled and shook her head. "I'll be right beside her."

Stephen and Solomon stepped up next to Tivona. Solomon held out his clenched fist, and Stephen placed his hand on it. Tivona and Leata did the same. Before any of them could say a word, Jess and Porty firmly placed their hands on top.

Gratitude welled up inside Will's chest as he joined

them, saying, "All for one, and—"

A bellowing voice came from inside Will's pouch, and the friends paused. "And one for all!" Laughter came from the united band.

Jess's mother looked on with admiration mixed with a deep motherly concern.

"I guess it is on to Sidar," said Will with a comforting feeling of camaraderie.

Chapter 22

As the trail to Sidar grew steeper and rougher, the travelers dismounted and walked their horses. Exhausted, they reached the top, but now an intimidating crossing loomed before them. Will gazed down at the river at the bottom of a very deep, rocky gorge. Then he shifted his gaze to the only way to cross: an old, rickety, wooden-slatted suspension bridge in desperate need of repair. One false step or rotten slat breaking beneath their feet would send them to their certain death.

"What should we do?" The wind blew locks of hair into Tivona's face, but it couldn't hide the worry in her eyes. "Doesn't look too safe."

Solomon approached the bridge and started inspecting the wooden walkway and the worn rope that held the bridge together. He grabbed the rope and shook it, only to watch one of the slats in the middle of the bridge shake free and fall the full depth of the gorge. It was too far down to hear it splash into the river. He turned to Jess. "Do you know of another way to Sidar?"

Jess shook his head. "Few people make this journey, and fewer have returned."

Stephen stared down into the deep gorge. "I don't know. This doesn't look good."

Will trembled inside. The life of his band rested on his shoulders. His white horse, Reggie, nudged him once and then again. Will glanced down at the ground, where Reggie's hoof stroked the tall grasses, and an object grabbed his attention. It was a blue fuzzy rabbit's foot like the one Sam always kept in his front pocket. He picked it up.

"What is it, Will?" asked Leata.

"I think this is Sam's. He must have come this way."

Jess nodded. "I guess that's our answer. Let me go first to see how safe this is."

Leata grabbed his arm. "Why are you going first? I'm lighter than any of you. I should go first." Tivona gazed at her sister with a look of anxious admiration.

Jess said, "I can't let you do that."

"Too bad you're not in charge." Leata led her horse onto the first slats of the bridge. They held up—so far—as she inched forward, testing each step.

When she reached the halfway point, she turned, and everyone held their breath. As soon as she let out the words, "I think we're good," one of the slats snapped, and she fell through, screaming and scrabbling for a handhold.

Will's heart leaped in his chest, and he lunged forward to the edge of the gorge, but Stephen held him back.

Clinging to the rope on one side of the slat, Leata dangled over a thousand-foot drop. Her horse peered down, seeming as concerned as her sister and mates.

"Hold on, Leata," Will shrugged away from Stephen's grip and stepped onto the bridge, feeling out each slat. "Hang on, Leata! I'll be right there!" Will reached the bridge's midpoint, grabbed the suspension rope, and knelt to reach out his other hand for Leata. "Hang on as tightly as you can and grab my hand."

Leata's eyes were wide with panic, but she followed Will's directions. She gripped the shorter, frayed rope tighter and reached for his outstretched hand. As hard as she tried to stretch, their hands were at least six inches apart.

Her arms trembled. "I don't know if I can hold on! My arm is getting tired."

Eyes locked onto her hand, Will tried to stretch further but couldn't.

"I'm losing my grip," she cried weakly.

"Hold on," encouraged Porty.

Will's horse nudged his arm and lowered her head, her bridle brushing against him. Without thinking, Will grabbed her harness and found himself able to reach lower. He gripped Leata's arm just as her other hand slipped. With a great heave, he drew her up. His horse helped, slowly backing up and raising her head to lift Leata's suspended weight from its dangling position.

Leata climbed onto the bridge, her sister's sigh of relief so loud they could all hear it. "I guess I owe you one, now," she said to Will, still catching her breath.

Relief coursing through him, Will only smiled. "I'm not even going to respond to that. I'm just glad you're okay."

They proceeded across the remainder of the bridge, and the others followed. Porty made his way, and then Jess crossed next. Stephen and Solomon stepped onto the rickety structure last. As Stephen neared the end and Solomon reached the middle of the bridge, large birds approached the area.

Anxious for his friends to reach safety, Will ignored them at first. But then he did a doubletake. "Stymph birds!" he shouted.

Porty shook his head. "Oh, no. I'm beginning to hate those guys."

Will called out to Stephen and Solomon, "You need to hurry."

But the birds swooped in too fast, and the first one cut right through the heavy rope with its razored feathers, while the second sliced through the other side, dropping the starting point of the bridge. Stephen's horse galloped toward safety. Stephen grabbed the slats in front of him, clinging onto them for dear life as the bridge slammed into the side of the gorge. Solomon did the same, his attention on the horse he was fond of desperately trying to grab the bridge but dropping into a free fall.

Stephen and Solomon dangled from the bridge that was now only attached at one end.

Jess and Will held Tivona's legs as she reached down to grab Stephen's hand and pulled him to safety.

Stephen shook his head. "I must climb down to get him. Hang on, Solly. Please hang on. We can get you."

Suddenly, the slat Solomon held cracked. It broke away in what seemed like slow motion. He frantically reached to grab another slat with his free hand, but a Stymph bird swooped down and cut cleanly through it.

Stephen screamed, "Noooooo," as he watched the friend he loved spiral down behind his horse.

Will didn't hesitate for a second. With no time to count or be stingy with his remaining wishes, he shoved a hand into the pouch and grabbed the goblet.

Just then, two Stymph birds soared toward him and sliced across his arm and chest, dropping him to the ground. Trying to wave them off, Will almost slipped over the edge.

Stephen and Jess drew their swords to strike back, but more flew in. Tivona reared back her bow and shot an arrow into the side of one bird, dropping it from its attack path. Suddenly, more were attacking them, focusing on Will as he frantically tried to reach for the goblet. Time was of the essence, and they were outmatched.

To the surprise of everyone, Will yelled with authority,

"Grab your horses and jump!"

As the number of deadly birds attacking them multiplied, Will grabbed the reins of his horse and plummeted over the edge. The others followed, and soon they each fell into a spiral toward certain death . . . as hundreds of Stymph birds swarmed high above. With air swooshing around him and the ground drawing closer, Will stuffed a hand into the pouch and grabbed the metal goblet, pleading, "I wish a safe escape for me and all of my friends!"

Squeezing his eyes shut and his friends' screams in his ears, Will readied himself for a crash landing on the rocky landscape or in the shallow river below.

In the next instant, his body struck water, and he submerged into eerie silence. Holding his breath, he opened his eyes. Dark blue-green water surrounded him, much deeper than he'd expected. He kicked his feet and swam upward toward the light from the surface, hoping he'd make it to the top before drowning. With a final effort, Will broke through the water and sucked in the air. One at a time, heads shot up from the surface: Jess, Stephen, Porty, Leata, and then finally, Tivona. Will held his pouch above his head to ensure Stitch and his family could breathe. Then, the horses each reached the surface. Not seeing Solomon, Will panicked and turned, splashing, looking all around.

A voice came from the shore. "I thought you'd never get here." A dripping-wet Solomon and his horse stood safely on the river's edge. He waved at Will and then reached out to help Leata ashore. "I wouldn't recommend it, but that was quite an experience."

Stephen made his way toward Solomon and hugged his soaked body. "Am I glad to see you alive! How the heck did we all survive that fall?"

Solomon nodded to indicate Will. "I guess we have good friends to count on."

Stephen glanced at Will through squinting eyes as if curiously trying to understand Will's power.

They followed the river shore to the town of Sidar, all the time watching out for the Stymph birds that continued to hover above their trail. Night had fallen by the time they reached the city. Will lifted his chin to see if a bright star hovered above.

There it was, as bright as the ones he saw above Lydia, Eppita, Sumara, Perggia, Thytira, and now Sidar. He would've felt disappointed if the star wasn't there. Could Sam be looking up at the same star? Maybe even Jules and Arrie were too. He missed all of them more than ever.

Chapter 23

Despite the nightfall, the city of Sidar bustled with activity, locals strolling the streets and visiting taverns like the one Jess led them to. They stepped inside through swinging doors to a busy saloon similar to those in the Westerns Will used to watch on rainy Sunday afternoons at home. The Sidar locals—short and stout with thick beards and bushy eyebrows—didn't look like cowboys, though. Finding most of them about Sam's height, Will suddenly felt tall.

"Why are we here, Jess?" Leata scanned the room.

Jess looked around too. "I'm hoping to find someone who might be able to help us with our mission."

Stephen followed his gaze. "Who's that?"

"She works in the back room, but you can't just go in to see her without an invitation, which she doesn't always give." Jess headed toward the bar. "Let me see what I can do."

While Jess inquired with the bartender, the rest of the group forged their way to the bar and watched the motley crew of characters. A short, hairy man approached Will and inspected him from head to toe. "You're not from around here, are you?"

Will hesitated, not sure how to answer, and shook his head. "Nope. My first time in Sidar. My name is Will." Glimpsing sudden movement from the man, Will clutched the pouch protectively; then, he realized what the stranger was doing.

The man stuffed a thin brown cigar into his mouth and lit it, puffing several times. "You can call me Troddie.

People are a little suspicious—jumpy, you might say—these days when they see strangers in town."

Solomon stepped forward. "Why's that?"

"Things have been happening lately: strange weather, a funny colored moon, and dead fish in the river. Just spooking people a bit," replied the man whose presence was much larger than his size.

Solomon asked, "What do you think it means?"

"Don't know, but people sense something big is about to happen, and uncertainty is uncomfortable for people. You know what I mean?"

"I do, Troddie. I'm Solomon. Hey, let me ask you another question. Did you happen to notice a man with a young boy in town that you haven't seen before?"

Troddie took another long puff, a stream of smoke swirling from his mouth. "Maybe, but I couldn't tell you where they are now."

Will leaned in. "What about a young girl and boy dressed kind of like me?"

"And me," added Porty.

Troddie smiled at Porty and then let out a deep, gravelly laugh. "That I would remember."

Jess returned and introduced himself to Troddie. He had been to Sidar many times before, so he was likely used to these creatures. He turned his attention to Will. "I spoke to some people. Sybilla can give us fifteen minutes to help find your family and friends."

"Who is Sybilla? How can she help?" Will watched Troddie squinting while taking another deep puff off his cigar.

Jess replied, "She's like a prophetess or an oracle. She can see things that we can't. I told her nothing, but she asked that Will, Tivona, and Leata be the only ones to enter the back room. You don't question Sybilla if you want her help."

Will's hand trembled as he turned the doorknob to the back room, where a saloon muscleman stood guard. The door creaked open to a dark room lit only by a small low-burning candle at the center of a round table. An old woman sat on the opposite side of the table. She wore her hair tied back with a colorful bandana, gold and silver beads around her neck and wrists, and a loose-fitting purple top over her round torso. Her emerald-green eyes seemed to glow in the dim candlelight.

"Sit down." She gestured with an open palm toward the chairs.

Will started to sit. "I need to know—"

"I will do the talking," interrupted the woman with a firm voice.

"But how will you know—" blurted Leata.

The old woman put up her hand. "You are here because I know. You are looking for someone. Someone very close to you."

Will nodded.

"Your brother and someone you did not expect to see-" She put her hand over the flame but did not flinch. "It is your father! You are also looking for your father."

Will nodded again.

"I can see a man with a young boy. They will not be in Sidar for long."

Leata leaned in. "Where—"

But the woman raised her hand again, stopping her. "I can see two other people dressed as yourself."

Though Will was suspicious of the woman, he started to feel more hopeful.

"Something is stirring the pot that has been simmering

for a long time, and it is about to boil over." She held a hand to her forehead and the other back over the flame. "It will not happen here but very close by. There will be storms, pestilence, an earthquake, and death. The sun will be blotted out, and the moon will turn red. Something powerful is going to happen." The woman began to tremble.

Will kept his eyes glued to her.

She opened her eyes and stared intently at each of them. "There are seven scattered cities of the old kingdom. That is how someone wants to keep it, but if they remain divided, they will die, each from a deadly cup. A large battle will take place in the seventh city marked by the brightest star. The evil one will lead one side into battle with tremendous force, and the scattered cities will not be able to defeat him unless they unite under the king chosen to reunite them."

Leata leaned forward, unable to contain herself, and blurted, "Who is the chosen king?"

One eye only shifted as the old woman gave Leata a piercing stare. "You must know this: his hands will not be bound."

"What does that mean?" Will said. "Who is he?"

"No one knows his identity yet. *He* does not even know. He will not feel worthy, but without accepting the mantle, the seven cities will be crushed forever and become slaves of the deceitful one and his forces. You will find the people you are searching for tonight." She waved them from the table.

Will got up to thank her, but she put her hand to her lips to silence him.

As they turned to leave, the door opened, and the woman let out an eerie sound. Her long, crooked finger pointed at all three of them. "The chosen one, the king, is someone known to you. Someone you trust and care about."

The candle suddenly went out, immersing the room in complete darkness. Finally, the bodyguard outside the door ushered them back to the raucous saloon.

"What just happened?" Leata's eyes opened wide.

Tivona shrugged. "I don't know. Why did she ask us three in, and which one of us was she talking to at the end? Which one of us would know and care about this chosen king?"

Stephen spotted the three of them and approached. "So, what did you find out?"

Tivona gazed into his eyes.

"Why are you looking at me like that, Tivona?"

"Just checking." Tivona smiled, but Stephen squinted his eyes.

"She didn't tell us where anyone is," Will said as the group gathered round, "but she did say that we'd find them in Sidar."

Leata quickly added, "She also said there would be a major battle, the good versus evil kind, in the next city, and a king would be chosen to bring together the seven scattered cities—and we'd know who it was!"

"Shhh," whispered Tivona to her sister as she peered around the room, her gaze lingering on Troddie.

Will studied Troddie a moment too. Could they trust him or anyone in this town?

They found no sign of Will's father or brother at the tavern, so they broke up into pairs. One of the tavern regulars stopped Tivona and offered her a drink on the way out. When he didn't take "no" for an answer and grabbed Tivona's arm, Stephen stepped in and made it clear to let her go. Leata seemed quite amused by how her sister admired Stephen's gallantry, even though she could have handled the situation herself. She smiled and exchanged glances with Jess and Will.

Stephen paired up with Tivona, Jess with Leata, and Solomon with Will and Porty as they scoured the city for any sign of Sam, Will's father, Jules, or Arrie. They checked with the local inns and taverns and questioned people they met on the street, but no one had seen them.

Hours passed with no luck, and Will was losing hope of finding Sam while strangely relieved about postponing meeting his father. He was beating himself up for feeling so conflicted. He had missed him for so long, but he had also been angry at him on many occasions for abandoning them. Knowing now that he may have had a good reason for being absent didn't make any of those feelings disappear.

They all met back at the tavern, and the news was the same: no leads, no clues, no luck. Will pulled out his leather book but found no additional messages to keep him from succumbing to hopelessness. He was tired. Trial after trial, city after city, with no visible sign of Sam.

Leata lifted Will's chin and opened her mouth to speak as if ready to offer words of encouragement, but a voice rose from behind. "So, you just got yourself some new friends to replace your old ones?"

Chapter 24

Will turned at the familiar voice, hope exploding in his chest.

There stood Jules with her hands on her hips, a smirk on her face, and Arrie next to her.

Without thinking or hesitation, Will took three long strides and put his arms around her. "Jules, we've been searching for you everywhere."

"Well, there's one place you didn't look." Arrie grabbed Will's shoulder, and then Will hugged him as well.

With a tear in his eye, Will laughed. "I know. We looked everywhere except for where you were. I can't tell you how happy I am to see you both."

Jules whispered in Will's ear, "And who's your new lady friend?"

Will's cheeks burned. "Oh, sorry. This is Leata and her sister, Tivona. And these gentlemen are Stephen, Solomon, and Jess. They've all been incredibly—"

"How quickly we forget our oldest friends," bellowed Porty as he stepped out from behind Solomon.

"Thank goodness, Porty!" said Jules. "We couldn't believe it when we lost you. The Four Musketeers are back and with reinforcements!" She put out her fist, and Will, Arrie, and Porty put their hands on top—and then everyone else joined in. "All for one, and—"

"One for all," finished Will, Arrie, and Porty.

Jules said louder, "And?"

The others joined in with a rousing "One for all!" Then everyone laughed and personally introduced each other.

Will moved closer to be heard over the loud, crowded

tavern. "Jules, we believe Sam is in town."

"That's great! Where is he?"

"We haven't found him yet. We've been all over the city with no luck." Will's despondency returned. Then someone tapped on his back, and funny looks colored the others' expressions. Will turned to see the culprit.

Sam stood behind him, grinning from ear to ear.

"Sam! Sam!" Will picked up his brother in a bear hug. "I've missed you so much." He suddenly realized how devastated Mom would have been if he'd never found him. With tears in his eyes, he finally put him down and rubbed his moppy head of hair. "I can't believe it."

"Sure you can; I'm right here. Guess what else?" he asked with a raised brow.

A tall man came up behind him ... the man in the photos at home. The man in the painting at the palace in Perggia. The man who was his father.

He gazed into Will's eyes with a fondness that only came from love and a longing heart. His eyes were kind and full of tears. When Sam stepped aside, his father approached Will with a half-smile and outstretched arms. "Is this *my* Will? Is this my grown-up son?"

Will put out his hand to shake his father's, but his father wrapped his arms around Will and hugged him tightly.

"Are you okay?" his father said. "I can't tell you how much I've missed you, Sam, and your mom. Tell me how she is."

Will buried his face in his father's jacket and breathed in the scent of the man he hadn't seen in a decade. "Dad, I can't believe we found you. I can't believe you're real. Mom's good. I hope she's not worried about us. I know she misses you so much."

"I miss her too. I missed seeing you two grow up. I

missed playing soccer with you. Who are all your friends here?"

Will's thoughts hitched on something his father said, but everyone stood waiting for the introductions, so he made them and explained how grateful he was for their unconditional friendship.

"I thank each of you for protecting my son."

Solomon stepped forward and bowed. "Your Highness. We have never met, but I am from Perggia, where you are king. It is an honor to meet you."

"Yes. Perggia has been very kind to me, and I hope I have been as kind to them. When I crossed over and survived the wilderness, I searched through each city for clues as to how to get back to my family. I found none, but I found a home in Perggia. Life is full of surprises, and I was humbled by the appointment to lead that great city. Now, I am honored to make your acquaintance. Thank you for befriending my son and helping bring him safely to me. You can call me William."

Solomon inquired, "King William, what brings your travels to Thytira and now Sidar?"

"We came after Jules and Arrie here and hoped to find Will. But I have another reason for this journey: I haven't told anyone yet. All the signs point to their being a reckoning for the entire kingdom in Philidopheos. The seven cities are scattered and lost, but they will now face all-out destruction if they don't unite to defeat a powerful force. I feel called to go there to fight for Perggia and possibly the great kingdom."

Will glanced through the tavern window at the night sky; the moon had turned crimson red. The sight sent a shiver down his spine, as the battle ahead would be very real.

Jess approached William. "I feel the same thing and would be honored to travel with you to Philidopheos."

The others agreed without hesitation.

Stephen said, "We will fight, and we will not give in!"

Inside, Will was not feeling as brave. He had finished his quest, finding both his brother and his father. His friends were back with him. Shouldn't they return home now? He glanced at the goblet inside his pouch, which showed the number *4*. It wouldn't be right to bring his younger brother into danger. He had vowed to bring him home safely. Who could he talk with to solve his dilemma?

Dad draped an arm around Will's shoulders, his other arm around Sam. "I can't believe we're together, but we aren't out of the woods yet. To get back home, we must find the portal."

Will tightened his brow. "A portal? How are we going to find that?"

"It's taken me ten years to find it, and that path has led me to Philidopheos. We must go there to find our way back home to Mom. I know it's a dangerous time, but it's the only way. I also don't think I can leave until I finish the mission I'm being called to. I could never have a clear conscience if this kingdom of seven cities is destroyed because I left."

Will nodded. "I understand. I also need to trust and not let fear stop me from doing the right thing."

"That's my son. We'll get an early start in the morning."

Chapter 25

At the large wooden table, Leata sat next to Will while they ate dinner with the others at the tavern. "How are you doing, Will? A lot's happened today."

"I feel like I'm in the middle of a tornado, and there's no way out. I should be feeling great, but I don't. How about you?"

Leata sighed and hushed her voice. "It's been interesting, to say the least. I'm glad you found your family and friends. I care about you and wanted to see that happen, but I'm still trying to figure out the puzzle."

"What puzzle?" whispered Will, noticing Jules glancing over at them.

"I keep thinking about what Sybilla, the oracle or whatever she is, said to us."

Will furrowed his brow. "She said we would find my brother, father, and friends—and we did, so why is that bothering you?"

Leata scanned the crowded tavern and leaned in closer to Will. "Not that part. The part about a king being chosen to fight the battle against the evil one and finally bring the kingdom back together to unity and greatness."

"Oh, right, but why are you thinking about that?"

Leata whispered, "She said that one of us would know that person, and it was someone we cared about."

"Huh. You're right. Do you have any ideas?" Will glanced around the table.

"A few." She smiled.

"A few? Like whom?"

"Well, Tivvy wonders if it's Stephen. Joshua certainly

thinks Stephen will wear a crown and has an important role in the upcoming battle. Plus, I get the feeling that Tivvy cares about him. I mean, not like the boy she thought was her true love, but I think she might be taking a chance again to like someone."

"What's up with her true love?" asked Will.

"It's a long story, but she was really in love with him, and we all thought he was very much in love with her—I mean, we knew he was, but then he disappeared into thin air. She's never gotten over it. Maybe Stephen can help her move on."

"Huh. Any more candidates?"

"Yeah. Jess is a prince and comes from the bloodline of a king. His mother, the queen, seems to think he has a calling to something great, and she prophesized this battle for the kingdom's survival," replied Leata.

"And you care about him?"

Leata blushed. "Well. Maybe a bit. But I have another candidate. Your father."

Will nodded. "He sure seems called to play an important role in Philidopheos, where he said this would come to a head. I can't believe my father could be the king of this kingdom. It seems too weird."

"But you care about him, right? And there's one more possibility." Leata paused and smiled.

"Yeah. Who's left?"

"You."

"Me?" Will blurted too loudly, drawing the attention of everyone around the table. "Me?" he whispered.

"Why not? You will have visited all seven cities, and the Taker seems very interested in you. Didn't you say that he's been on your case the entire journey?"

Will let out a long sigh. "He has, but that doesn't mean I

could ever be the chosen king."

"Then why is he so preoccupied with you?" asked Leata.

"I don't know, but Sybilla said that one of us knows the person and cares about them. Who cares about me?"

Leata kissed him on the cheek. "Didn't you hear me tell you that I did?"

With that, Jules got up and walked over. "Ahem." She cleared her throat. "What's with all the whispering over here?"

Will stood up, more embarrassed than anything else. "Umm. Nothing. We were just playing a game."

Jules whispered in Will's ear, "Since when have you played kissing games?"

"No, no." Will waved his hands defensively. "Leata was trying to figure out who the mystery king might be. That's all."

Jules laughed. "Oh. That's easy. It's you." With that, she walked away and sat back with Porty and Arrie.

Will was left shaking his head and laughing at the thought of it.

With an apple in his hand, Sam got up from where he'd been sitting with his dad and ambled over to Will. "What's so funny, Will?"

"Nothing. How're you doing, little brother? I haven't had a chance to really talk to you." Will put his arm around Sam.

Sam smiled. "Maybe I should disappear more often."

"So, what happened after you disappeared in the attic?"

"Um. I fell onto some green flowers and walked for a while until everything turned misty and cold. It was pretty scary, and then I met this man who asked if I needed help. I told him I was lost and wanted to get back to my family. He touched my head and said that he might be able to help."

Will was confused. "Who was the man? What kind of help?"

"He didn't say, but I felt I could trust him. When a large bird flew down, the man said it could take me to a safe place. Then he helped me onto the bird's back, and it took off. I mean, I was really flying." Sam's face lit up. "It was high and scary but kind of cool too. We were in the air for a long time, and it was dark when we landed. When I got there, a palace guard took me in and gave me warmer clothes and a place to sleep. When I woke up in the morning, Dad was looking down at me."

"Dad?" asked Will.

"Yeah. I didn't recognize him at first, but he seemed familiar. Then I remembered the photo in the living room that Mom often looks at. I've always wondered what Dad would look like in real life, and there he was. I said, 'Dad?' and he nodded. It's been great spending time with him. Then, one day, I saw Porty in front of the palace and called out his name. He told us all about you, Arrie, Jules, and him trying to find me. That's when Dad said that we had to go searching." Sam bit into the red apple.

"That's unbelievable. Maybe someone *is* watching over us. I was worried sick about you the whole time." Will rubbed his brother's hair. "But we've got to get some sleep for tomorrow."

As they stepped outside, William came over to the boys. "I still feel like this is a dream. I'm really with my two sons. All we need is your mother to make us a family again. I promise we'll get back once the kingdom is won. Sound like a plan, sports?"

They both nodded, but Will was ready for some serious sleep before heading to the final city. As he stared at the night sky in the direction of Philidopheos, it didn't take long to find a bright star overhead, just as he had seen over the other six cities. This star, however, seemed more brilliant than the others. It made Will shiver and wonder what lay ahead for them. Why would they risk heading into what could be the battle of all battles, even if it were the only way to get home?

Chapter 26

Will's heart raced as he tried to run from a giant beast clawing at him from a black mist. His legs felt like two bars of heavy lead in quicksand, leaving him hopeless and panicked. He recoiled as it grabbed his shoulder... and he jumped.

"Will, Will! It's okay. You're just having a nightmare."

Will opened his eyes to see his father's comforting face and the sunrise glistening in the background.

"You okay, son?"

Will rubbed his eyes, realizing it was a dream. Sam was still sound asleep next to him. "Yeah. I'm okay. Are we leaving now?"

"Soon. I'm hoping we can get you and Sam back home before the day is out," replied his father.

Home. Will flung his covers. He relished the word. He couldn't wait for him and Sam— "Wait! What about you?"

"I'm hoping I can join you soon, but I can't run away from my responsibilities here. Sometimes we must put doing what's right ahead of our own wishes. If we are called to be there for others, we must answer that call. Does that make sense, Will?"

"I guess so, but—"

"Will, this is too important. I must do this. Wake up Sam in a few minutes, and I'll see how the rest are doing."

An hour later, everyone who planned to head to Philidopheos met under a large oak tree: William, Will, Sam, Solomon, Stephen, Tivona, Leata, Jess, Porty, Arrie, and Jules. Will checked his pouch to see that Stitch and his family were all accounted for.

William gazed at each of them. "I'm moved that all of you are willing to make this journey to Philidopheos at such a perilous time. First, I must ensure my sons and their friends get home safely through the portal. Then, I need to prepare for the battle of battles for the resurrection of this once-great kingdom. Our adversary is powerful, but I have forces coming from Perggia to help. I want to give all of you a chance to change your minds and return to your families."

They all shook their heads at the offer to leave.

Solomon clenched his fist. "We are all part of this kingdom, even if we have been separated by fear and selfishness in the past. If we do not fight this foe, all hope will be lost. We would have nothing to go home to."

Stephen put his hand out. "I am ready to fight to the end."

Jess put his hand on Stephen's. One by one, each person did the same.

Finally, a hairy hand with stubby fingers landed on top. "No one is going anywhere without me," bellowed Troddie, who had surprised everyone—showing up to travel with this small, possibly doomed, band of warriors.

A few hours later, they reached Philidopheos, a humble, less sophisticated city of one-story homes and buildings with thatched roofs.

"This place is a lot different from the other cities," Will said.

Solomon scanned the area. "This city always remained more faithful to the unity of the kingdom and the Giver."

Will followed his gaze, struggling to picture an epic battle between good and evil. "Do you really think the battle will be fought here?"

The town sat on a high hill. Solomon pointed to a large

field that stretched out below it. "That field is called Meggio. Many important battles have been fought there in the past."

In Will's imagination, he pictured the clashes between two great armies in that field, but it seemed too peaceful now to think of one about to happen. *Maybe everyone was wrong,* he thought, and then he remembered the red moon in Sidar. Was that a sign of the blood soon to be poured out on this meadow?

As they neared a little market in town, Porty rubbed his belly. "Let's find a food vendor."

"Yeah, I'm hungry too." Will picked up his pace. What little food they'd packed for the journey had gone quickly, so he hadn't eaten in a long time. Will shuffled up to a table that held seven unique pottery bowls.

The man behind the table turned to Will, but his eyes were closed as if he were blind. He cried out, "Be true and righteous, or all will be lost!"

With a gasp, Will stepped back.

The man waved his hand over the bowls for sale. "You wish to buy one?" His hand caught the last one, which dropped and smashed on the ground.

"Oh, let me help you." Will stooped to pick up the pieces.

"You are kind, but I can take care of this." He waved Will back.

As Will backed away, he glanced at the man's face and winced.

Sores covered his face, and his eyes opened, flashing fire—like the beast Chimera.

Still in shock, Will stepped further back and bumped into his father.

"Will, what's wrong?" He hunched over Will.

Will turned back to the man, pointing, but the sores had vanished, and all seven bowls sat unbroken on the table.

"Nothing." Will shook his head. "The hot sun must be getting to me. I need something to drink."

"There's a fountain in the square with cool water from the river." His father pointed.

Will went to the fountain, still feeling the sun's heat on his brow. As he cupped his hands to take some water, another bowl smashed on the ground. Ignoring the incident, he attempted to drink the water slipping through his hands, but it turned crimson red as if mingled with blood. Sickened at the sight, he opened his hands and shook them dry. But when he looked back down, only clear, clean water bubbled up in the fountain. Still, he dared not drink it. Instead, he returned to the blind man selling the pottery.

The man said, "You need to repent and trust the good, or you will always be thirsty. Trust in the good and do not be taken in by the deceiver."

Will backed away in fear.

"Are you okay, Will?" His father grabbed him by the shoulders and turned him around. "What's wrong? You are acting strange."

"Nothing. I-I'm fine. Let's go." Will glanced again at the blind man, who continued preaching repentance. "I promised Stitch we would try to find the rest of the Kiggles who have been rounded up. This is the last place we can check where they could be held captive. Are you okay with that?"

William hesitated, then gave a fatherly smile. "Sure. Let's try to find them."

"Thanks." Will rejoined the others.

Two men came up the hill, pulling a cart. One of the vendors said to them, "Where's your fish today? Your cart is empty."

One fisherman trembled as if terrified. "They're dead.

They're all dead."

"What's dead? What are you talking about?"

"The fish in the river. All the fish are dead!" the fisherman shouted.

Before anyone could reply, the sun turned black, casting a shadow over the city. Anxiety filled Will's chest.

"What's happening?" a woman shrieked, shielding her eyes.

William stepped forward, hands raised. "Everyone, please listen and remain calm." People began to circle William and the others. "We've seen signs for some time that the evil one is planning an attack, a battle. Philidopheos has been considered the most likely place for this battle because you have been the most faithful people in the kingdom and because, throughout history, many major battles have taken place here. This is not the time for panic but for coming together in strength and resolve to remain faithful."

A man yelled out, "When will this happen? How will we be able to fight the Taker?"

Another woman pleaded, "How will we be able to recognize him?"

William held out his hands again as people began shouting more questions and concerns. "These are all good questions. Some believe that there is one chosen to lead you in this battle to victory. A new king for the kingdom where all seven cities will be together again."

"Who is this king?" a man cried.

"No one knows, only the Giver. But I can tell you that the chosen king is within the walls of your great village. If you trust and follow him, you will see victory at the end of the battle." William lifted his fist into the air.

"How can we follow him if we don't know who he is? Does *he* even know who he is?" asked a round woman who had pushed her way to the front.

"You must trust that it will become clear to you. Have confidence in this king's ability to lead you and defeat the enemy for good. If you stay together and never give in, all will be well," said William.

A man stepped toward William, squinting and looking him over. "I've seen you before."

"I've not been here for a long time." William eyed the man directly.

"Are you from Perggia?" he asked.

"I am."

"Are you not the King of Perggia?" he persisted.

"I am," replied William.

"King William of Perggia, we are honored that you come to Philidopheos at such a dangerous time. You bring calm and hope to a nervous group of people who don't know what to expect. Are you not the king that can lead us?"

Will watched his father gaze across all the faces in the large, growing crowd. "I cannot answer the question yet."

"But you may be our king, the leader who will save us?"

William didn't respond but nodded to the man. "We must wait for clearer signs."

Chapter 27

They paired up to search for the Kiggles. William went with Sam, Will with Jules, Porty with Arrie, Leata with Jess, Tivona with Stephen, and Solomon with Troddie.

As they ambled through the narrow streets of the humble town, Jules bumped Will with her shoulder. "I'm sorry for giving you a hard time last night. I guess I was a little jealous."

"Jealous?" Will shook his head. Why would Jules be jealous?

"Never mind. I've been worried about you since we split up." Jules tilted her head as her eyes fixed on him.

"Tell me about it. I was going crazy with worry. Luckily, many people helped, even though some scary things happened along the way. The book kept leading me on. *Go this way. Trust and be brave.*"

Jules asked, "How many wishes remain on that friend of yours in the pouch?"

"On the goblet?" Will scanned the area to ensure no one watched as he pulled out the goblet. The number *4* was etched onto it. "I need to be extra careful now that we'll be facing even greater danger."

Jules closed her eyes for a second. "Do you think your father would keep you here during a war? Didn't he bring us here to find our way home through the portal?"

"He did, but he says he cannot go until the battle is won. He says he couldn't live with himself if he were the reason the kingdom was destroyed."

Jules raised her brow. "Huh. Does he think he's that important? Do you think—? Never mind."

"I think that he suspects he may be the one called upon. He's been to all seven cities in the kingdom. He is already a king and obviously a leader. He calmed those frightened people in the square, maybe proving he'd make a good king, leading his people in calm and unity. I guess anything can happen here."

"Wow. That is something. If you brought Sam home, would your dad follow you after he's finished?"

Will shook his head. "I want to protect Sam, and you guys shouldn't be involved, but I don't feel like I can leave my father behind. How would he get back without the goblet?"

"That's what I admire about you, Will. Your trust, loyalty, and bravery." Jules gazed at him.

Will found himself smiling. Jules admired him? He couldn't think of anyone who had admired him before. Maybe Sam did because Will was his older brother, but Will didn't deserve it.

After several hours of asking people and checking into buildings, they still hadn't found any Kiggles. So they headed back to their agreed-upon meeting place in the town square. As they walked, Will opened the pouch and peeked inside. Stitch and his family gazed up at him. "We won't give up. Maybe one of the others has good news."

His brow furrowed in concern , Stitch nodded.

Each team came back to the square without any good news.

Stephen studied the people gathered in small groups, the simple buildings, and the nearby marketplace. "Not a single lead, but I can tell you that people are very nervous. They're looking for someone to bring them together. They want to know what's going to happen."

Jess nodded, then said with conviction, "It's up to us to

help organize and prepare the people for whatever comes. Leaders don't wait; they lead."

Leata stood smiling at Jess, a look of admiration on her face. Then she said, "Remember, Sybilla told us—"

Will caught her attention by shaking his head, so she stopped short.

"Oh, that we should do what Jess suggested. We need to come up with a plan," she added.

Troddie grunted, "Reinforcements will be coming from Sidar. I don't believe this will be a minor skirmish. The signs tell us we are close, so we must prepare the troops here for battle."

William nodded. "I think Stephen, Jess, Leata, and Troddie are all correct. I've already talked to the mayor and captain of the volunteer army. They are preparing their people and could probably use our help."

Sam rested his hands on his hips. "We didn't even find any Kippers."

"Kiggles," Will said with a half-smile.

Tivona stepped forward. "We need to be wary of being misled or deceived. I don't think this will be a battle of physical weapons alone."

Solomon nodded.

Will dropped his head, running his hand through his hair. "What if the signs are wrong, and a battle isn't coming?"

Before anyone could reply, the earth shook and got everyone's attention.

William's eyes widened. "These signs are real, Will. We can't ignore them." William strode out into the square, and people began gathering, likely worried about a more significant tremor.

"King William, what are we to do?"

He waved the crowd closer, making it possible for people to hear him. More people flowed into the square and stood quietly, waiting for him to speak. The anticipation grew as Will's father waited for everyone to pack into the square.

William climbed onto a granite platform and waved them closer. "Great people of Philidopheos. As you can see, the signs are coming more frequently now, and we must be ready to protect our homes and defeat the enemy. We must vanquish the Taker completely, or the kingdom will be destroyed. I say this so you all know how important it is to remain calm and work together. I have spoken with the mayor and the captain of your soldiers. They are making the necessary preparations so we will be ready. They need your support."

A cry came from the middle of the crowd: "Are you our king? The one chosen to lead and protect us?"

William scanned the crowd. Most wore expressions of anticipation and hope.

Will stared directly at his father. He could tell that his father wanted this. He had told him earlier that he believed it was his calling to be the king and save these people from evil.

The crowd began to yell, "William! William! William!" Their chant grew louder and louder as more people joined in.

Will turned to Jules, Arrie, and Porty, who were now chanting with the crowd, but Will was reluctant to join in.

Suddenly, the ground rumbled under their feet. The people quieted and looked up at William.

"The time is growing closer." William pointed downward to the Meggio Valley and at the sight of the enemy troops rallying. A few exclamations of panic spread through the crowd, multiplying with every passing second until he held up his hand. "Panic is what he wants. His weapon is to divide us. We must stay united and strong."

An old woman dressed like a gypsy said, "This battle has been a long time coming. We need a young male sacrificial offering to protect us as we fight. He will be revered throughout history for sacrificing himself for the kingdom."

Disturbed by the old woman's words, Will turned to his father to catch his reaction. "What is she talking about?"

William sighed deeply and crouched down to whisper to Will, "I'm not comfortable with this, but we will never have the support we need in this fight without offering a sacrifice. It's one person out of so many across the kingdom, a life that would have been lost anyways without it. I can't change it, and I'd be putting everyone at peril if I tried to. The woman must select the boy. Sadly, my hands are tied on this."

Will drew back, horror bringing a scowl to his face. "What? You never said anything about a sacrifice!"

Fear overtook the townsfolk, shrieks, and panic rippling through the crowd.

Then, one man shouted, "Let's build the platform for the sacrifice!"

Men and women dispersed, soon returning with wood and furniture from the buildings surrounding the square. Others fought over the furniture, breaking everything apart, and then they placed the broken pieces onto a growing heap for a bonfire.

Shaking his head, unsure what to make of all this, Will backed up and bumped into his brother.

The old woman moved past Will, turning her head so that the wart on one side of her long nose showed. She scanned the crowd through squinted eyes. Women shrieked as her gaze traveled toward them, and they attempted to shield their sons from the old woman's sight. But she seemed able to tell where each child stood anyway as if she didn't rely on her sight. She crept sideways, tilting her head as she inspected possible candidates, and the crowd moved back from her.

Another strong tremor shook the ground under their feet. Everyone looked down into the valley, where many soldiers and animals, all in black, gathered for an attack. This was no longer a future threat; it was happening now.

The old woman stopped and leaned closer to a boy. The parents pulled him back. She moved to the next and the next until she made a complete circle. Then the gypsy turned, and her long, crooked finger pointed directly in front of her. The crowd parted, moving to each side of the path of her pointed finger. She shuffled forward deeper and deeper into the crowd until her finger and deadly stare settled on one young boy.

Sam.

"No!" Will shrieked, rushing to his side.

"This is the boy," said the old woman in a coarse voice. "He must be the one."

Will turned to his father. "You have to do something!"

"Son, I told you my hands are tied. I cannot change this."

A sneaky suspicion had wiggled into Will's mind, and now he was certain. He drew his sword and leveled it at his father. The crowd let out a gasp. "Leave now, or I will plunge this into you!"

"Leave our king alone. We need him to fight," came a cry from the crowd.

Determined. Unwilling to back down, Will stared into William's eyes.

William—not William—returned a twisted smile. "You cannot s-s-s-ave S-S-S-Sam."

Gripping his sword in his sweaty hands, Will plunged it into William's heart but found no resistance to his blade. William's body turned into a black swirling mist.

"You may think you are clever, Will Donovan, but you can only s-s-s-save yourself by bowing down to me."

Will slashed his sword in vain through the black mist as it rose above the frightened crowd.

"Think about your families. You will not s-s-s-survive. Your families-s-s-s will perish unless you bow down to me as your king!" bellowed the voice from the mist as it drifted off.

Suddenly, the ground shook so hard that a large crack opened through the center of the village. The earthquake rattled the buildings, making some collapse, and people screamed in terror.

Will stood on the edge of the precipice created by the quake. On the other side stood Sam, visibly frightened as the townspeople moved toward him—the sacrifice that promised their safety.

"Will!" screamed Sam with outstretched arms.

Without hesitation, Will backed up and leaped over the six-foot-wide gap in the earth. He landed with one foot on the edge and the other frantically searching for a footing. Then he slammed to the ground and tried to grasp the dirt as he slid over the edge.

Stephen dove for him, grabbing Will's hand just before he dropped to certain death. "Hang on, Will! Hang on." Jess and Troddie grabbed onto Stephen and helped pull him up, but the strap of the leather pouch slipped from his shoulder . . . and the pouch dropped toward the void.

"Stitch!" Will shouted, twisting to watch the pouch fall over the edge. Devastated, he dropped his face to the dirt, and tears streamed from his eyes.

Sam, on his knees, wrapped an arm around Will's head and buried his face in Will's hair as if to comfort him.

"Will!" yelled Solomon from the other side of the crack. He stood with Leata and Tivona, who held her bow in one hand.

Will lifted his head and turned toward Solomon, who pointed into the wide crack. Not sure what Solomon wanted to show him, he got up and approached the edge with Sam, Stephen, and Jess. About five feet down, the pouch hung from one of Tivona's arrows.

She smiled and lifted her bow. "I saw the pouch slipping off your shoulder. Luckily, I'm a quick draw."

"Hold on, Stitch!" Relief almost made Will giddy, but he had to stifle a laugh. First things first. "We'll get you." But how could he get them without falling in?

Sam tugged his sleeve. "I'm the lightest one. Lower me down."

Will shook his head. "I can't take that chance."

Sam smiled. "It's okay. I can be brave, too."

Stephen and Jess held Sam's legs and lowered him with his arms stretching for the pouch, but it was just out of reach. "I need to go lower," he yelled upward as a growing crowd watched him dangle. Finally, his outstretched hand grabbed the strap of the pouch.

"Hang on," shouted Will. "Hang on tight! And I mean you two, as well," he said to Stephen and Jess.

They pulled Sam and the pouch to safety. In the meantime, Solomon, Tivona, and Leata had found a narrower spot to jump over and joined them.

Will lifted Stitch and his little family from the pouch to ensure they were okay. "Sorry about that." Will exhaled, happy to see them alive.

Stitch shook his head. "No more thrills for us today, okay?"

Will smiled and scooped them into the safety of his arms.

An old man stood among the group which had formed around Stitch and his family. "Kiggles, huh? There're more of them in town, you know."

"What?" Will turned back to the man.

"There's more of them. I've seen them." The man pointed at the Kiggle family.

Stitch's ears perked. "Where have you seen Kiggles?"

The man smirked. "I don't know where they are exactly, but I saw someone bring them into town several days ago."

As the man shuffled away, Will said, "We've got to get Sam away from here before they try to sacrifice him."

"What's a sacrifice, Will?" Sam cocked his head to one side.

"I'll tell you later."

They huddled around Sam and ushered him out of the crowded square, still shaken by the earthquake's devastation. The enemy armies had grown and were moving across the Meggio flatland below. As the group hurried along, a woman yelled, "Look!"

Will drew closer to Sam, fearing for his safety.

She cried out again, pointing over Stephen's head. The image of a jeweled golden crown with a crimson-red skull cap hovered above him. "It's the sign! He is our chosen king! Our savior!"

Tivona stepped back. The crimson crown image hovered squarely above Stephen's head. "Stephen, is it you?"

"Is it me, what?" Stephen asked, turning to look around.

"Are you the king your father talked about, the one Sybilla told us would be chosen? Is this the sign?"

Chapter 28

Stephen glanced up and all around, apparently stunned by the questions and everyone pointing to something over his head.

Will's eyes widened at the sight, thinking back on Stephen's father's beliefs about his son. Will turned to Tivona and Leata. "What do you guys think?"

Leata leaned in. "Everyone claimed a king would be chosen. It makes sense that the time is now. Sybilla said it would be someone one of us knows and cares about." She glanced up at Tivona. "And you care about Stephen, don't you?"

Tivona stared down as if deep in thought.

"Tivvy, you like Stephen, right?" Leata stepped closer.

Tivona shook her head. "I don't know. I thought I might, but I don't know. I mean, I care about him as a friend, but—"

Will tilted his head to see what was in Tivona's eyes. "But what?"

She didn't respond.

Leata nodded with a smile. "You still haven't gotten over him, have you?"

"Who?" Will looked from one sister to the other.

"Her true love. Her best friend and soulmate. Her David. He left and never returned, but she still loves him," answered Leata.

A tear escaped from Tivona's eye.

Leata wrapped her arm around her sister. "Well, you only have to care. Sybilla didn't say anything about having to love the king."

The people packed in around Stephen and Solomon while Jess continued to shield Sam. "Are you our king?" they asked again.

Solomon leaned toward Stephen. "This is no time to freeze up. Joshua has thought this for a long time now. Maybe he's been right?"

Stephen turned to Solomon as if finally taking in the possibilities.

Will held his breath, waiting for the answer. Solomon was right; this was the time for leadership to emerge.

In the next moment, Stephen was up on a platform, peering over the people's heads, gazing out at the mounting armies below heading toward them. "I don't know the answer to your question," Stephen shouted, "but I do know that this is a great city in what should be a unified and glorious kingdom. We are not divided because of anyone but ourselves, putting our personal goals ahead of the whole. Philidopheos has been the most loyal city, and you are a good people. That is likely why the deceiver is making his attack here."

Stephen scanned the crowd. Everyone seemed to hang in anticipation for his next words. "I don't think we can defeat him—" Their expressions sank until he added, "We can't defeat them alone. But we are not alone. We have the Giver on our side. We have goodness, decency, and truth on our side. We have—"

Suddenly, a hundred short and hairy soldiers entered the square in full uniform. Troddie stepped forward. "And we have some of the bravest and fiercest soldiers from your neighbor, Sidar!" The crowd cheered. Troddie smiled and saluted his soldiers, and then he turned to Stephen. "You didn't think I'd come to a battle empty-handed, did you?"

Hope rose in Will.

Stephen smiled and turned to the crowd. "I believe in you. I believe in this kingdom. We need to believe in and trust the Giver and be willing to courageously give our all to defeat his enemy—once and for all!"

Another rousing cheer came from the crowd. Tivona watched him with glowing admiration, her look suggesting that she might actually care for him as more than just a friend.

"Today, we prepare. We prepare our homes and our weapons. Our battle is against a deceiver who represents everything we are not!"

With a final cheer, the crowd dispersed. People headed toward their homes to get ready, appearing confident; they had their king and believed that the Giver was on their side. Troddie led his soldiers from the square to find the most strategic spots to protect.

The group of friends remained in the square: Will, Sam, Solomon, Jess, Tivona, Leata, Stitch and his family, and the new king, Stephen. After a few conspiratorial glances, Will and the others stepped back and bowed formally to Stephen.

He shook his head but couldn't hide his smile. "Very funny. They'll be no bowing here. We've got some serious planning to do. That doesn't look like child's play going on down in the valley."

Stephen squeezed Will's shoulder. "Will, you showed courage and bravery in your quest to save your brother—and a lot of love. I'm proud to know you."

Will felt heat flush his face at the compliments, knowing he had just acted on instincts and almost got killed in the process.

"I have one question for you, though," Stephen said.

"What question?"

"You aimed a sword at someone we all thought was your father to save Sam. How did you know that William wasn't your real father?"

Leata added, "I was wondering that myself. I thought you had lost it when I saw you draw your sword. What gave you a clue? He seemed so gentle and attentive to you and Sam."

Will put his arm around Sam. "Well, my whole life, I've dreamt of finding my father one day—imagining how I would feel and what he'd be like in person instead of in my head. As kind as he seemed to Sam and me, I never felt the connection I imagined I would. At first, I thought that might be normal since we didn't really know each other, but something didn't seem right. He talked about playing soccer, and I never played soccer when I was little; I always played baseball. My Poppie—I mean, my grandfather...was called William. My mother told me that my father was called Willy, and I was Will, but he called himself William. He did ask about my mom, but he never asked about Poppie, not once."

Leata's brows shot up with a surprised expression. "That was enough to stick a sword in your dad? Well, your fake dad?"

Will shook his head. "No. Those were just questions. But Sybilla told us the person chosen to be king would not know it and would be humble. He seemed to want it, yet there were no signs he was chosen. She also said that his hands would not be bound. When the people wanted to sacrifice Sam in the fire, he didn't try to protect him at all. He kept telling me his hands were tied. At that moment, warnings went off inside me, the way they had in the barren swamp when the Taker tried to deceive us.

Besides, it always struck me as odd that Sam was mysteriously taken directly to him. Then I remembered that the Taker was the ultimate deceiver, and my gut told me this was him trying to take Sam. I wasn't going to let that happen." Will pulled Sam closer.

Sam peered up at Will. "Does that mean we'll never see our real dad? I wanted to believe he was real and that we finally had a dad."

Although his heart ached for Sam's loss, Will smiled. "I know. At least we're together here." Thankful for his friends, Will turned to make eye contact with each of them. "Wait a minute. Where are Porty, Arrie, and Jules? They're not here?" He couldn't spot them anywhere in the square. Had the Taker whisked them away in his black cloud to be used for his own purpose in the brewing battle?

Will spotted the rubble from a building toppled by the earthquake; panicked, he rushed toward the pile. "Jules! Arrie! Porty! Can you hear me?" Will waited but got no reply, despair creeping back into his heart. "I can't have lost them again."

A muffled voice came from underneath the pile. "You're not getting rid of a musketeer that easily."

"Porty? Is that you?" Will drew near.

"Let me check," said the voice with a long pause. "Yep. Sure is."

"Are you okay? Are you hurt?"

"My leg is caught under a beam with some heavy pieces of stone on top. I don't think it crushed anything. I'm just stuck. I'm getting hungry too."

Will smiled in relief. "What about Arrie and Jules? Are they okay? Are they with you?"

"They went to get help. The quake opened the floor of

this fallen building, revealing tunnels below," Porty said. "They've been gone a while now. I hope they're okay."

"Hold on. We'll figure something out."

In the next moment, something zipped over Will's head . . . a flaming arrow. It pierced the lone upright wall of the building.

Stephen yelled, "Will, stay here with Tivona, Leata, and Sam. Solly, Troddie, and I will see to the troops. We'll send help if there is time, but they are moving quickly below."

"Okay!" Will turned back to Porty. "Porty, we'll find a way to reach you. Don't give up."

Porty replied in a muffled voice, "I think I hear Jules. They're back."

Relief coursed through Will. The sound of rocks scraping about came from the other side. Grunts, groans, and more scraping of stone against stone.

Tivona waved Will over. "Let's move these beams. I can hear them on the other side!"

Will ran to her and grabbed the end of a beam, but its weight and size made it hard to lift. Large chunks of stone and concrete held the beams in place. Should he use a wish? No, the actual battle might demand something from his goblet.

Even with the four of them—Will, Tivona, Leata, and Sam—they barely budged the large beam. Stopping for a breath, Will looked at the leather-bound book for possible guidance. New writings filled a page: *The battle to come will be deadly and relentless. It will take the courage of many and a martyr's sacrifice to save the kingdom, but all must trust that they do not fight alone or in vain. Remain faithful and push past your fear. May you be strengthened by an old wish and a true king that lie beyond these stones.*

Will thought about each word. An "old wish" and a "true king"? He rarely understood the messages in the book until they started to unfold. He had to trust.

Will put the book away. "Let's try again." When Will grabbed the beam this time, it budged and lifted.

Leata laughed, looking as surprised as Will felt. The friends all helped, and together they pulled the heavy beam from its wedged location. They dragged boulders aside to the sounds of people doing the same on the other side until, finally, an opening formed. Will pulled a final stone away, and Jules crawled out first.

Grateful to find her safe, Will gave her a hug. Arrie came next, and then Porty.

Porty smiled. "I told you I was okay. It's good to be out, though. Luckily, Jules and Arrie found help."

Will turned to Jules, who raised her hand. "Arrie and I found this labyrinth of tunnels underneath. They must run underground throughout the city. The earthquake damaged the wall of what looked like a dungeon where prisoners were kept."

Just as Arrie stepped away from the opening, a man, likely in his twenties, climbed out. His ragged clothing, unkempt hair, and dirty face couldn't hide his strong features. As he made his way off the rubble heap, Tivona grabbed Will's arm as if needing it for support, and she exhaled. She watched him with teary eyes before finally finding her voice. "David!"

Leata turned, and her jaw dropped. "Oh, my gosh! What?"

Will looked from Leata to Tivona. "What is it?"

"It's David," Leata whispered. "Tivona's heart and soulmate who had deserted her—or so she thought. I thought he must be dead." She strode closer as if to make sure it was him. "Are you David?"

He squinted for a moment then recognition showed in his eyes. "Leata? Is that you?"

She nodded, putting her hands to her mouth as if wrestling with disbelief. "It is you! Tivvy is here."

He scanned the surroundings. Leata stepped aside, revealing Tivona, who stood behind her. They both cried and embraced without a word for several moments until David held her shoulders and stepped back as if to drink the sight of her in—a sight he may have dreamed about for years now. "I missed you so. How did you happen to be here?"

Rather than answer, Tivona kissed him and let him hold her again.

Standing next to David, Will responded, "Tivona and Leata ended up here because they came to help me. Then they realized the help this city needs—it's about to face a battle with the Taker—so they and all of us are preparing to fight him."

"Amazing," David said.

"Oh, and my name is Will Donovan." Will offered his hand.

David shook it. "Good to meet you, but I have some news for Tivona and Leata." Before he could say another word, another man emerged from the rubble. He was a generation older than David, with white hair and tattered soldier's gear.

Tivona dropped to her knees and placed both hands over her mouth, but it couldn't quiet her emotional reaction. "Oh, my gosh. Father! Is it really you?" She got up and rushed to take his hand, helping him descend the rubble pile. Then she hugged him tightly, and tears flowed down her cheeks. "How can this be?"

"My name is Saul," Tivona's father said to the others. He touched Tivona's cheek and reached out for Leata.

"I could hardly remember what you looked like," she said through tears.

He pulled her close. "It's been far too long to be without my precious girls. I can't believe how you have grown so beautifully."

Leata said, "But you went to war, and we thought you died."

"Ah, I did go to war to protect our city of Eppita, and without my family, I did feel dead at times. When we lost our fight, we were taken prisoner in Perggia by the evil one who was falsely acting as the king." Saul turned to David and grabbed his shoulder. "This courageous young man tried to rescue me and almost made it. He's been imprisoned with me and many others considered a great threat to the evil one." Saul looked at Tivona with misty eyes. "He's a good man, your David. I am proud to know a man of such character, courage, and strength, which I have not seen the likes of in any other man—and he loved you enough to risk his own life to find your old father."

Tivona's hands shot to her chest as if her heart were bursting. Then she hugged him again. "We missed you both so much and tried not to lose hope. I wish we had a way to let Mom know."

Saul surveyed the valley. "It looks like we have some work to do before we can return home. We have heard rumblings and seen signs of an epic battle about to happen."

More men emerged from the opening in the rubble pile, one after another, dirty and worn, but each with a look of conviction in his eyes.

The group brought them to the walled edge of town, where they could see the black forces progressing up the hill. David's eyes narrowed, jaw tensed, but he also stood taller, as if formulating a strategy that gave him confidence.

In the next moment, arrows rained onto the square.

David said, "We have about a hundred and fifty men motivated and willing to fight. We need to get to the armory, hold the entry points to the city, and fight them on the slopes to maintain an advantage."

Troddie returned with a few of his men and broke out into a wide grin when he saw the additional soldiers ready to fight for the kingdom. "They're coming from all sides. This area looks like the most vulnerable."

David scanned the valley in front of him. "He's right. Their backs are to the east, which will be their attack focus. We will need more weapons and men in this area."

Suddenly, a giant bird swooped down toward David.

Before Will could yell to watch out for the razor feathers of the Stymph bird, Tivona brought down the attacking creature with an arrow to its heart, dropping it with a loud thud to the ground.

As it lay there motionless, Leata smirked. "And more women."

David nodded in gratitude to Tivona and then returned Leata's smile. "I'm thoroughly impressed, and I'm sure you have a few tricks up your sleeve as well."

More and more men climbed out of the tunnel. Troddie's men brought them swords, bows, and spears for the fight.

Will kept Sam close as he watched the men in tattered clothes prepare to fight the deceiver who had imprisoned them for so long and taken them from their families. Will knew well that the Taker threatened to destroy the families so dear to these men who had never lost hope. While happy that Tivona and Leata had found the father they thought they'd lost forever, sadness teased him. He and Sam had had only the false promise of an imposter.

Stephen and Solomon returned on horseback to the square to find the men arranging themselves in position. Both Will and Sam approached them.

"Where did you get these men? I was concerned that only Troddie's soldiers would be holding them off from this side," said Stephen.

Will replied, "The earthquake created an opening to a tunnel network under the city. One tunnel led to a prison holding many of the Taker's enemies. He had held them in Perggia and brought them here to keep them under guard, but the quake took down the walls, and they escaped. Even better now—Saul and David were among them."

Stephen's brow furrowed. "And who are they?"

"Saul is Tivona and Leata's father. They thought he was lost at war."

"That is amazingly awesome," exclaimed Stephen, accompanied by a broad smile from Solomon.

"And Tivona's boyfriend too!" shouted Sam.

Will whacked his arm.

Stephen's shoulders drooped. "What?"

Will said, "David was a friend of Tivona's and went searching for Saul years ago. He was imprisoned with Saul until now. I think Tivona thought they were both lost forever."

Stephen spotted Tivona and approached her. Before he

could say anything, David came from the other direction. Stephen's eyes lifted, and his eyes widened. "David?"

Tivona glanced from David to Stephen. "You know him?"

"Sure. We used to ride together. My father knew his father," answered Stephen.

David smiled at the sight of his boyhood friend. "You're looking good."

Stephen smirked. "And you seem a bit ragged and dirty, but I'm sure you'll clean up fine. I heard—" Just then, a series of flaming arrows soared above their heads.

David clutched his friend's shoulder and made ready to move on. "We'll have to catch up later. We have a battle to fight. Who's leading this fight?"

"Stephen is the chosen king. We saw the red crown above his head." Sam waved his hand over his head. "That's how we know."

David nodded and bowed humbly. "Then let's win this war."

A rush of adrenaline ran through Will's body as he prepared to join in.

Chapter 29

Over the next few moments, black clouds rolled across the sky, and a haunting mist filled the air, making it hard to see. Saul called for his daughters and Will, Sam, Jules, Arrie, and Porty. "War is serious and dangerous. Take shelter in the tunnel as they mount their attack."

Tivona grabbed his sleeve. "Dad—"

He held up his hand. "I know what you want to say, and I admire your courage and heart, but I want you to do as I ask." His eyes told her that arguing with her father was not an option.

Will approached Saul. "Sir, can I talk to you alone?"

"Will, we don't have time right now—"

"I understand that you want to protect your daughters, and I realize the rest of us are young, but I think all this has something to do with me. I think the Taker is coming directly for me, and I don't want to run anymore. I can't have other people fight my battles while I hide. Does that make sense?"

Soldiers stood in position at the wall. On the other side, dark-haired beasts dressed in armor and wielding giant swords spewed fire from their angry eyes. They hurled themselves at the stone walls, soon crashing through. Then, they easily cut down the defenders of good.

Saul glanced at Will. "He comes for all of us, especially when he spots a weakness, a selfishness. If you want to help me, take my daughters, your little brother, and your friends to safety. Please do that for me."

Just then, a beast raced toward him. Saul spun toward it and swung his sword, striking it down with a tremendous blow. "Go now!" he yelled at Will with a desperate look of resolve.

Will raced back to the others, standing near the rubble pile, and grabbed Sam's hand. "Let's go! You're all with me," he shouted, ushering his friends into the underground tunnels.

He dropped down last. Flashes of light came from above, along with the sounds of fighting. Tunnels carved out of underground limestone led in every direction. Which way should they go? His father—the imposter—had said something about a portal. Was there really a portal here in Philidopheos?

"Not fair." Tivona stomped her foot and folded her arms across her chest. "Banished like a child to the safety of the underground!" She glanced down one dark tunnel and another, then turned to Jules. "Where do these tunnels lead?"

"When we first discovered them, we followed that one with the lit torches." She pointed. "We wanted to find help for Porty but then came upon the prison."

They followed the dark, damp tunnels, stopping where they branched off, unsure how to proceed and wondering if another earthquake would bury them forever. Finally, they reached the tumbled wall to the prison where Tivona's father and David had been held. She turned and smiled as she saw The Four Musketeers standing side by side in their costumes. "It looks as if the prisoners all got out. Let's keep going."

Sam said, "Hey, can you hear that?"

"What?" Will focused on the sounds around them.

"Listen." Sam held up a finger and stood motionless as if trying to determine the faint sound's direction. "I think it's over there."

Everyone moved closer to the wall Sam indicated. A scratching sound came from the other side.

Will picked up a jagged stone and struck the wall, cracking the hard surface. He struck it repeatedly, loosening a large stone until they could move it back and forth. Soon, it came free. A single flame cast a dim light on the other side, revealing a large dungeon room. The scraping sound was now louder.

Stitch yelled from the pouch, "Lift me up, Will. Lift me up. I know that sound!"

Will scooped Stitch up and placed him upon the opening.

Stitch made a sound Will had not heard before. "Eeeutha, eeeutha." The sounds on the other side of the wall became louder. "It's them!" Stitch yelled louder into the dark hole. Suddenly, a tiny figure appeared in the opening. A Kiggle!

Will helped them down as more and more appeared. "Stitch, your friends. We found the captured Kiggles! Wow, so many."

A few minutes later, at least one hundred Kiggles freed from bondage stood on their side of the opening. One of them leaned in to whisper in Stitch's ear. Stitch stepped back. "There's more."

Will peeked through the hole. "More Kiggles?"

"No, more prisoners on the other side of the back wall to this room," relayed Stitch.

They worked furiously with stones to break through the wall, thrashing harder and harder until cracks grew into holes. The thumping echoed on the other side as they pounded against the hard stone. Then a rumble of voices came from the other side, and hands grabbed and pulled pieces down to widen the hole. Soon, the prisoners on the other side came into view and pulled themselves through the opening.

The first man's face appeared, covered with years of grime and mistreatment.

Will drew back. Scores of Kiggles gathered behind him. Had they just let out a dangerous criminal, or was he a falsely accused prisoner of the Taker?

The man's narrowed eyes and careful movements showed him equally leery of them. "We have seventy-five men in there. Thank you for getting us out. Who are you all?"

Will introduced everyone and said, "A major battle is going on above ground. The city is under attack by the Taker's forces. He aims to destroy Philidopheos and the kingdom."

"I'm not surprised. That monster has been rounding up the people he fears most for some time now. You say the battle has already started?"

Tivona said, "Yes, and they need all the help they can get."

One by one, the men crawled out of the opening. Will hoped they could find their way to the surface through the winding tunnel maze, up through the trap door, and into the palace. Sam remained in the tunnel with the Kiggles and Porty while Will and his companions joined the freed men.

They found an armory room with weapons, but the heavy door was locked. Luckily, there was an opening that Stitch could manage, and he unlocked the door from the other side. They grabbed their weapons and headed to the plaza to assess the fierce battle.

Will's eyes bulged at the spectacle against the darkened sky. Beasts of many kinds had broken through the city's walls and were attacking the soldiers of Philidopheos, who weren't prepared for the sheer number of enemy attackers, the viciousness of their blows, and the blood being spilled.

Surprisingly adept at wielding their swords, spears, and other weapons, the freed men charged without hesitation into battle to reinforce the overwhelmed townspeople. From the palace steps, Tivona began making shot after shot with her arrows, taking down the hideous beasts on land and in the air. Will drew his sword and turned to Arrie and Jules, who did the same.

Jules nodded. "Does not the merit of all things lie in their difficulty?"

Just then, a hairy beast with fire in his eyes came up behind her, ready to crush her.

Will reared back and flung his sword into its chest.

Jules' eyes narrowed until the creature fell with a loud thud, and the ground rumbled behind her. She nodded, then turned and swung her sword at a smaller but no less menacing creature, dropping it in its tracks.

Arrie yelled out, "Go, get 'em, Jules! What was the line in the book we were reading in class?"

Jules smiled. "It is only the dead who do not return."

"Let's make sure we all return," yelled Arrie as he charged an enemy creature preparing to strike one of the town's soldiers.

"Look out," yelled Will as a large flaming object came hurling over the city wall. It landed to the side, injuring several townspeople.

Porty stepped onto the battlefield, visibly shaken. "This is real! Watch out," he cried, pointing as a Stymph bird swooped down.

The bird suddenly dropped. Tivona had shot him

through the heart.

"Thanks," said Porty, tipping his cap to Tivona.

"What are you doing here, Porty?" Will shouted above the mayhem. He'd left Porty with Sam in the tunnel. "Where's Sam?"

"That's what I came to tell you. I was checking out a noise, and when I stepped back, he was gone. The Kiggles must have followed him, but I was suddenly alone and didn't know what to do."

"I can't lose him again, Porty! I've got to find him." Will turned back and swung his sword, severing an arm from an attacking beast and then finishing the beast off with a lethal jab.

Jules yelled out, "It might be a trap. You can't go alone. We are The Musketeers, and we stay together."

"Okay." Will turned and stopped in his tracks, stunned by what he saw in the distance near the palace entrance.

"Will, what is it?" asked Jules.

Will opened his mouth but could think of no reply. Could his eyes be deceiving him?

"Come on, Will, we have to go!"

Will forced himself forward, toward the figure in the distance, unable to shake himself from the trance-like state, wanting to believe . . .

Porty shouted, "Grab Will. I think that evil character has him spooked."

As Porty and Jules each grabbed an arm and tugged him along, Will could not break his gaze from the figure. They drew nearer, the battle raging around them barely registering.

Will remained frozen as the man took his spear and hurled it toward Will, missing him by a few inches.

Wide-eyed, Will followed the spear's path and saw it

strike a fierce-looking creature behind him squarely in the chest. Will looked at the man again. He'd saved Will's life.

The man took several long strides and grabbed Will by the arm, pulling him to the stairs of the palace entrance. "This is no place for a boy. Take your friends to safety if you care about them."

Will stared at him. The man had unkempt hair, a dirty face, and threadbare clothes . . . he was one of the men freed from the dungeon. Will didn't respond nor take his eyes off the man as Porty, Arrie, and Jules joined them on the steps.

The man pointed to Leata. "Ma'am, take your friends to the underground. This is only going to get nastier."

Porty said, "Will, we need to find Sam."

The man stopped and turned to Will. "Who are you? Why are you staring at me?"

"Will Donovan, we've got to go!" Porty yelled louder as a ball of fire landed to their right.

The man's jaw dropped as he gazed into Will's eyes. "Will?"

Will nodded, and his tears flowed. He didn't try to stop them.

"Will, is it really you?"

He nodded again and closed his eyes as the man hugged him. Will buried his head in his chest while Tivona landed several shots to protect them from enemy attacks.

In the next instant, the man hurried Will into the building, and the others followed.

Jules clutched Will's shoulder. "Who is this man? How does he know you?"

Will replied, "*This* is my father. I don't know how I know it, but it's him."

The palace foyer was quiet compared to the battle going on outside. Will's father stooped a bit to peer into Will's eyes. "How did you know it was me? You were only three when I left."

"I just know." Will wiped his wet cheeks.

Porty narrowed his eyes. "How do we know he's not an imposter again?"

Chapter 30

Will's father stood with him in the battle-torn palace foyer. "What's this about an imposter?"

Before Will could explain, the dark swirling mist reappeared and made its way toward him. "Will, none of you will s-s-s-survive today unless you care enough to s-s-s-save them."

Suddenly, a massive creature with black scales, fire in his eyes, and six-foot-long claws appeared behind Will's father and sliced through his back.

"No-o-o-o!" Will screamed. "No!" He gasped, and horror rippled through his body.

But his father dropped with a thud to the floor as the creature withdrew his bloody claws.

Will stood in disbelief. He hadn't even had a chance to talk to him. Fury raged through Will. He gripped his sword with two hands and swung it at the black swirl of mist. "I will never, ever bow to you! I will never trust you!"

The mist swirled upward with a disturbing laugh and disappeared.

Will sank to his knees, clutching his father's body. Tears flowed, and his heart ached. All those years of longing to see his real father again, to be with him, to play with him, and now he lay lifeless on the marble floor. He felt disheartened that the Giver hadn't protected his father. He was abandoned all over again.

Suddenly, a muffled sound reverberated from underneath him. Will got up only to realize the sound had come from the pouch. He was squeezing Stitch and his family without thinking.

"Sorry, guys." He opened the pouch and checked on them. They stood on either side of the goblet.

The goblet! Will lifted it from the pouch and held it in both hands, staring at the number *4* now engraved on the front. Closing his eyes, he concentrated on the metal cup in his hands. "I wish time would go back so my father was alive again." It was a wish he felt deep in his soul that needed to come true. He waited a moment, then opened his eyes.

The crowd watched, but nothing happened. His father remained lifeless on the floor, and the sounds of the enemy pounding on the palace doors were getting louder and more forceful.

Arrie grabbed Will's arm. "Will, we have to go."

"I can't leave him here. I can't," cried Will.

"I know how you must feel." Jules knelt beside him.

He leaned down and hugged his father's lifeless body, holding his head in his arms.

In the next moment, something smashed through a window high in the wall. Glass crashed and tinkled to the floor a few feet away, and a dark beast crawled in through the jagged opening. Its fiery eyes turned to them. More windows smashed, and more beasts crawled inside.

Jules got to her feet and dragged him up, too. "We have to get out of here! We have to find Sam."

He could feel her hand on his shoulder and didn't want to risk her getting killed too. Before he put the goblet back into the pouch, he pulled out the leather-bound book and hesitated before opening it. Then he found a single word on the next page: *TRUST*.

As they rushed toward the tunnel entrance, Leata

glanced to her left and right. "Wait. Where's Tivona? We can't leave without her."

Will looked at his friends. He needed to rise above his anguish and see to the safety of his friends. "Wait, Leata; I'll come with you." They dashed out the side door, back into the battle in the square. Then, they scanned the fighting soldiers under an even darker sky. Another Stymph bird swooped to the ground in front of them, the razor-sharp feathers barely missing them.

"There she is!" Leata pointed to her sister on the palace steps, who, after stopping the Stymph from attacking them, lowered her bow. Leata ran to her and explained the situation. The two then fought their way back to the rest of the group.

Just then, Will shuddered. The ghost of his father appeared near the palace entrance. Will shook his head and rubbed his eyes, but there the man stood, or *was* it his father?

Porty said, "Grab him. I think that evil character has him spooked."

Will stood stunned again, staring as he had when he'd first stood in this spot and seen his father. Porty and Jules each grabbed an arm and tugged him along.

The man fought off beasts with his spear, then he met Will's gaze, and as footsteps pounded the earth behind Will and his friends, his father's ghost hurled his spear toward them.

Will gasped, the spear just missing him. Then he followed the spear's path and saw that it had hit a creature behind him squarely in the chest. Hope teased him again. Could his wish have come true? Had time been reset? Yes, his father was alive!

The man took several long strides toward Will and

grabbed him by the arm, pulling him to the stairs of the palace entrance. "This is no place for a boy. Take your friends to safety if you care about them."

Will stopped him. "Dad. It's me, your son."

His father gave him a curious expression, which soon became one of recognition. And hope. "Will? Is it really you?"

As Porty, Arrie, and Jules joined them on the steps, Will and his father hugged, and Tivona protected them from enemy attacks. In the next instant, his father pulled him into the palace, and the others followed.

Jules clutched Will's shoulder, concern etched in her brow. "Who is this man? How does he know you?"

Will smiled. "I'll explain later. Let's go."

Chapter 31

Once safe inside the quiet palace foyer, Will's father peered into Will's eyes. "How did you know it was me? You were only three when I left."

"I just know." Will touched the hilt of the sword at his hip.

Porty asked, "How do we know he's not an imposter again?"

Will's father furrowed his brow. "What's this about an imposter?"

Will opened his mouth to explain when the dark swirling mist appeared. Again. Making its way toward him.

"Will, none of you will s-s-s-survive today unless you care enough to s-s-s-save them."

"Not again." Dread filled his chest as the same hideous clawed creature appeared behind his father. This time, Will was ready. Drawing his sword, he leaped forward and slashed through one of its claws.

As the creature moaned and thrashed, Will's father plunged his spear into its chest, and Tivona pierced its head with an arrow. The large frame crashed to the ground with a loud thump.

Will turned to the black mist and held out his sword. "I told you before that I'll never trust you or bow to you. We have a higher power on our side."

"Clever boy, Donovan." The mist drifted back. "You'd better take care of his s-s-s-safety, now, hadn't you? I wonder if S-S-S-Sam is s-s-s-safe too?"

Will's father turned to him. "Sam is here too? Where is

he now?"

Porty raised his hand. "I was taking care of him, and he seemed to vanish. He might be in the tunnel somewhere."

Will's father shouted, "Let's go before it's too late."

As they strode through the dimly lit tunnel, questions he'd always wanted to ask filled Will's mind. "Dad?"

"What is it, son?"

"First, I want to say that I'm sorry. Sorry for believing that you deserted us for all those years."

His father stopped and put his hands on Will's shoulders, looking him straight in the eye. "Will, I wasn't there for you. You deserved a father who could be there for you, teaching you and letting you know you were loved every day. I'm proud of the young man you have become, but you have nothing to apologize for. Do you believe that?"

Will nodded but still felt terrible for the awful things he had thought about his father at times, in between longing for him back. "What happened? Did you accidentally go through that wall in the attic?"

His father smiled as they walked side by side. "So you've been talking to Poppie, huh? I began to doubt him. He told me about an adventure he'd gone on, but he didn't tell me what it was or how he got there. He only mentioned that it started in the attic. I spent too many days searching for a clue in that attic when you were just a baby. I held that pouch hanging from your shoulder and found the goblet and book inside. The pages were blank, and the goblet looked like one of your grandfather's old trophies with a *10* engraved on it."

Will rested his hand on the pouch. "Dad, did you make a wish when you touched the goblet?"

Will's father exhaled a long breath, as if trying to

remember. "I don't know. Maybe I did. I was always saying that I wished I could find the secret passage Poppie talked about. I remember a strange sound, and I backed up against the wall. Next thing I knew, I was in an extraordinary land. And I just started wandering."

"Was it that back wall in the attic?" Will said.

"Actually, it was. Is that the portal?"

"Only if you made a wish. I'm guessing we'll need one wish to get back." Will pulled out the goblet and showed his father the number *3* that was now engraved on it.

"So you've used seven wishes so far?"

"Yeah. Not all intentionally, so I'm trying to be careful. I just used one in the palace square," replied Will.

"On purpose?"

"Yeah. I wished time would go back so that the creature with the claws wouldn't kill you again," said Will.

"What? You mean I died, and you saved me?"

"I think so."

"See? I knew I had good reason to be proud of you." Willy smiled at Will. "Thank you. Now let's find Sam."

They wound their way through the labyrinth of tunnel corridors, finding several dead ends. After some time, they reached the rubble where they had entered the tunnel, except now the entrance was blocked. They tried to clear the opening but couldn't budge the large stones.

Stitch yelled from the pouch, so Will let him out. "What is it, Stitch?"

"Is there a small opening I could get through to get some help?"

"There's a small one right there." Willy pointed to a speck of light.

Will lifted Stitch to the spot, and Stitch squeezed through. A short time later, scraping sounds came from the other side. The large stones shifted and slid until an opening formed, large enough for their escape.

Visible against the darkened sky, the battle seemed even worse than what they had experienced in the palace square, this time with shots from canons, the roar of enemy creatures, and screams from the townsfolk attempting to defend their homes. Stymph birds swooped over the battlefield, attacking in force, and the dark beasts outside the city walls breathed fire over the city, striking down one soldier after another.

Will scanned the battlefield. "Where's Sam? Can anyone see him?"

"I can't see him anywhere," Jules said. "Maybe he didn't come out of the tunnel but went back when he found the entrance blocked."

Something tugged Will's trouser leg, drawing his attention. Several Kiggles stood at his feet, so Will set Stitch down.

Stitch pointed to the opening. "They said Sam and the others made it through the tunnel before a giant threw a large stone, closing the opening."

Will's father said, "Where is he now?"

Stitch shook his head. "He seemed to have disappeared into thin air."

As Stitch lifted his hand to explain, everyone's gaze lifted to a great ball of fire hurtling toward them. Then they all ran for cover.

His father yelled, "Will, you and the others need to get to safety now! This is too dangerous."

Stephen approached from the battle. "No one is giving up, but it's not going well. We can't keep up with their numbers and fierceness. We've taken on a lot of casualties."

Just then, a beast charged them from the side, and Willy turned to jab his spear into its chest while Stephen landed a blow to its neck.

"We've got to get you guys to a protected area," said Willy as he scanned the area for cover.

Tivona argued, "But we need to—"

Will cut in. "We respect your position, but we will need everyone available to fight, or we will lose. If we lose, we will all die anyway. If you want to protect us, you'll let us help."

Stephen hesitated. "He's got a point, doesn't he?"

A series of large thunder rolls shook the ground as a giant climbed over the city wall. The giant almost stomped on soldiers in its way, but they fled from his path.

David and Saul raced toward it and lashed at his feet and ankles with their swords, but it only seemed to anger him more. He lifted his foot and flung them several yards into the air.

Will ran to help David stand up before the giant crushed him.

Stephen grabbed Willy's spear and charged the giant, and then launched the spear into his thigh, bringing a loud groan.

The angry giant bent down and picked up several boulders.

Stephen shielded Will and David, who were still on the ground.

Tivona yelled, "No-o-o-o-o!" as the giant reared back and flung the stones.

Stephen fell at the impact, and his body lay lifeless on the ground. At that moment, Will glimpsed a familiar face. Stephen's father, Joshua, climbed over the wall with several soldiers from Sumara, arriving in time to witness his only son fall in battle.

His face flushed with fury, David rose and grabbed a stone. Then, using a cloth belt from his waist, he slung the jagged rock directly at the angry giant, striking its head and opening a wound that gushed blood. The giant wailed as he turned dizzily, toppling backward and crushing several enemy beasts.

Beasts continued to scale the city walls in ever-increasing numbers, and the sky turned black as it filled with the dangerous Stymph birds. Joshua fought off the attacks and then lifted his dead son's body into his arms. Solomon reached out to touch him as if wanting to console his dear friend. David, Saul, Troddie, and now the others formed a protective circle around them, fighting off the enemies. Tivona struggled to keep up with the Stymph birds as they soared downward with their sharp feathers.

Will stood motionless as he watched Joshua holding his son. "Stephen was the king. He is dead, and the kingdom is lost."

Joshua stopped. "Will, Stephen was called to wear a crown, but not the crown of the king of this kingdom."

"What do you mean?" Will asked.

"The gold crown is for the king. He wore the martyr's crimson crown. He gave his life for the good fight and to protect the true king. He knew it, and he still chose to fight the evil one, to put love over self-interest, and to give his life for those he loved." Joshua and Solomon took Stephen underground, where his body could be laid down with respect, but Will felt paralyzed with confusion.

"Will!" shouted his father. "You can't stand there. It's

too dangerous." He swung his sword to slash an oncoming beast as Tivona dropped another bird that was aiming directly for Will's head.

"We have no king, and there are too many of them to overcome. What can we do?" implored Will.

"Fight!" yelled his father. "We must trust that we will win, and then we must find Sam."

The word "trust" shook Will. Hands trembling, he pulled out the leather book and opened it to find some guidance, some hope in what felt like a dark and hopeless situation. When he opened it to the next page, his heart dropped. The page was blank. He closed his eyes with the sounds of battle raging around him. He had come all this way only to face certain death and lose his family. When he opened his teary eyes and began to close the book, writing appeared one letter at a time. *Trust your instincts, Will. Never give up hope in fighting for a kingdom that is right and good and needs its king.*

Chapter 32

This was the first time the book addressed Will directly, by name. What did it mean? *Trust your instincts. Don't give up hope. The kingdom needs a king.* What was he supposed to do?

Trust your instincts. Will gazed up as the people of Philidopheos fended off a never-ending supply of enemy attackers. *What can I do? What would a king do? Am I supposed to be the king?* The thought frightened him.

Another ball of fire hit the ground to his right.

He shielded himself from the flying shards of fire, then noticed his friends—Porty, Arrie, and Jules—fighting frantically with their swords. And Tivona with her bow and arrows. He needed to move beyond the feelings of doom.

Trust your instincts. Will reached into the pouch and touched the goblet. He could feel the number *3* and let his instincts tell him what to say. "I wish—what do I wish? Okay, I wish for the kingdom to have its rightful king to lead this kingdom to victory over the enemy."

The battle raged on, nothing changed, and the sky grew even darker. More beasts broke through the barrier walls, including dragon-like creatures breathing deadly fire blasts. To his left, hairy beasts nearly overcame his father, and more beasts closed in on his friends. He closed his eyes and pleaded in his thoughts. *I won't give up hope. I will trust. I need to know what to do here. I need a sign. I trust you.*

A soldier approached Will. "You are Will Donovan. Am I correct? Do not give up hope. My name is Rekat. Trust me. I will never give up."

The soldier's words encouraged Will.

In the next instant, his father got to his feet and slayed the beast. He pointed and said, "Will, look!"

Joshua returned to the wall and waved to the men he had brought. Then he yelled to Will, "I'm not letting my son die in vain. We have five hundred soldiers from Sumara and another three hundred from Eppita."

David and Saul joined them as they began to push back the invaders, but the harder they fought, the more the number of beasts and Stymph birds seemed to increase. Will and Rekat fought to an opening in the city wall, where the spectacle of battle raged on the rocky hillside and into the meadow.

Just as Will's hope faded, trumpets blew in the distance. Two more cavalry units headed for the battle scene.

Solomon yelled, "We have reinforcements from Perggia!"

Jess stepped forward and pointed. "And the queen has sent soldiers from Thytira!"

Troddie slapped Jess on his back. "Well, it's about time. My men from Sidar have been here from the beginning. We desperately need all the help we can get."

The beasts continued to move up the hill, crushing the soldiers in their way. Even with the additional troops, they still faced an incredible challenge. Jess and Solomon rode their horses down the slope, slashing beasts as they descended. The enormous beasts, three times their size, reared back to crush them, and Tivona could not get a good shot from her vantage point. Leata screamed as one beast reached the men, but then the beast's legs went out from underneath him. Several other beasts began to fall.

The rocks on the slope were not rocks at all. They

turned over one by one and stood to full height; the Lydians were not going to miss this fight! Beno smiled and waved at Will before striking the feet of another beast.

Will smiled with a hope he had not felt all day. He turned to Jules, who stood beside him watching the spectacle. "Now, all seven cities fight together against a common enemy. United. We just need the true king to lead them to victory."

Jules turned toward Will, and her eyes grew as large as her smile, though she did not look directly at him.

He turned to peer behind him in the direction of her gaze. David fought alongside Saul at the wall, taking down another beast and stopping a swooping Stymph bird in mid-air. Above his head hung a gold crown. "Jules, David is the rightful king!"

She smiled. "And that's not all. It looks like we have a queen as well." She pointed toward Tivona. Twelve stars surrounded her head. Tivona returned a quizzical expression as Jules pointed above her. The trumpets sounded again, and David led a charge down the hill, pushing the beasts back into the meadow, where all the troops fought together, decisively turning the tide of the battle.

Will, Arrie, Porty, and Jules turned to each other and shouted, "All for one!" and charged down the slopes to join the fight until the enemy was defeated or retreated with the Stymph birds.

Each stood on the battlefield, smiling while trying to catch their breath in the break. Solomon consoled Joshua for his only son's sacrifice while fighting the darkness. Gradually, the skies brightened, overcoming the dark mist on the battlefield.

Will stood in disbelief. Was it finally over? Had they won the battle and reunited the kingdom at last? Will turned to Rekat, who had fought gallantly alongside him. "Rekat, we only just met, but thank you for fighting with such courage. You probably saved my life more than once."

Rekat smiled. Surprisingly, he was not breathing heavily and didn't seem tired. "Thanks, Will, but we've met before."

Will tried to remember an earlier meeting. "When was that?"

Rekat pointed to the square where the battle had begun, but Will still couldn't recall. As he peered up the hill, something hovered high above the square. It wasn't a Stymph bird or any type of bird at all; it was someone that Will couldn't make out.

"S-s-s-something tells me that you'll figure it out." Rekat's eyes turned a sinister red.

Will jumped back from him and bumped into his father.

"What is it, Will?" asked his father.

"The happy family, almost together again. S-s-s-sweet, isn't it?" hissed Rekat as he smiled and dissolved into an all too familiar swirling dark mist. "But where's S-S-S-Sam to make it complete?"

Will turned back to the figure hovering above the square. "It's Sam! Dad, that's Sam above the square." He and the others raced up the hill to the town's square. High above the opening in the ground, caused by the earthquake, some force suspended Will's brother, Sam, in the air.

"Will?" cried Sam. "I'm afraid!"

"I'm here, Sam, and so is Dad! We'll get you down. You'll be okay!" yelled Will.

"Listen to your brother, Sam. We won't let you fall." Willy searched their surroundings, probably looking for something to reach Sam. If Sam fell, it would be to certain death.

As the crowd looked on in horror, the black mist swirled overhead.

"Will, S-S-S-Sam is not going to be okay if you don't protect him—if you let him down. Do you follow?"

Fire shot up from the crevasse in the earth, directly below Sam, and the crowd gasped.

Will peered down into the pit of torturous fire and red-hot lava below.

David stepped forward with Tivona. He called out to the black mist, "Your evil forces have been defeated, crushed because all seven cities have united to fight together against you. We are committed to never being separated again!"

The voice from the mist cackled. "Let's us s-s-s-say that you have won a battle but not the war. I have an endless s-s-s-supply of s-s-s-soldiers to fight and defeat you whenever I want. Your arrogance can quickly be put in check."

The crowd buzzed at the words of the deceiver. Will's panic grew, but he wanted to calm his brother. "Dad, what are we going to do? We can't let Sam die."

"You don't have to let him die, don't have to cause your little brother's death—the one you wished would dis-s-s-appear," hissed the voice. "You can s-s-s-save him—if you really love him, that is-s-s-s."

"Will, I'm scared," cried Sam.

Underneath the panic, Will kept hearing the word *trust* in his head and heart. How was trust going to help him here? *Trust. Trust. Trust.* He repeated the word to himself in a frantic attempt to calm down. Then he reached for the pouch, but it was gone. Confused, he scanned the ground. "Where's the pouch?"

Will's father glanced around too. "What is it, Will? What are you looking for?"

"The leather pouch I got from the attic, the one with the book and goblet. I need it to save Sam and to get back home. I don't know what happened to it. I remember holding it when we ran up the hill," Will nearly screamed.

Without the goblet for a saving wish and the book to provide wisdom and guidance, Will felt alone and hopeless, but resolve soon replaced panic. He would save his brother, though he could think of only one way.

Chapter 33

The crowd stared upward with anxious anticipation as the voice from the swirling mist hissed, "It's up to you, Will. How much does-s-s-s your brother really mean to you? What are you willing to do to s-s-s-save him?"

Jules stood next to Will. "Be strong, Will. Don't let him lie to you." With that, a force struck Jules and knocked her to the ground, and Will dropped to her side to help her.

"You can s-s-s-save many people with a gesture of humility, Will. Don't let your pride get in the way of being a real hero. You need only kneel and honor me. Trust me, or this city will be destroyed, and S-S-S-Sam will be cast into flames-s-s-s. The choice s-s-s-should be an easy one."

Will didn't need time to think. He only had one choice. "Let go of Sam and leave this city and take me. It is me you have wanted all along, so I will trade myself for Sam." Conviction stirred inside Will. He had no choice but to sacrifice himself for his brother and fellow kingdom members. Stephen was willing to give his life for Will and David, two strangers. How could he not do the same for his own brother? "Take me and let Sam go."

The deceiver hesitated before hissing back, "Very interesting. I hadn't expected that of you, but it doesn't work that way. I want your s-s-s-submission to me. I want you to bow down and honor me. I have the power of life and death over you, your brother, and everyone here." The black mist expanded, and the crowd leaned back in fear.

Will didn't know how to respond. He would not bow

down to evil. But he wanted to save Sam and everyone else. Glancing downward, he noticed Stitch and his family behind a stone next to the crevasse.

Stitch shook his head, signaling for Will not to give in. He pointed behind him to where a hundred Kiggles stood together, holding onto each other's feet and hands, making themselves into a big Kiggle net. Stitch motioned for Jules, Porty, Arrie, and Will's father to edge their way over to where the Kiggles were gathered. Jules knelt next to Stitch and then leaned back toward Will, whispering, "Just trust."

Wanting to distract the mist, Will paced back and forth as if trying to figure out what to do.

"I am losing my patience, Will Donavan," hissed the voice.

Out of the corner of his eye, Will noticed Jules motioning to several people on the other side of the opening.

"I'm los-s-s-sing my patience, Will," he hissed again.

Will's father pointed up at the mist in anger. "You're nothing but evil. Why are you picking on my son?" An invisible power shot down from the mist and bashed Willy to the ground with a force so great it knocked him out.

Will dashed to him and knelt to see if he was alive. Then he looked up and yelled, "I will never bow down to you. I can't trust anything you say or promise. You're nothing but a coward and a bully!"

The voice grew deeper and angrier. "S-s-s-so, have it your own way!" As the mist moved away, Sam screamed—no longer suspended above the burning opening, he fell. Will ran to the crevasse as Jules, Porty, and Arrie grabbed onto the Kiggles, who had created a crochet-like blanket with their bodies. They whipped it across the crevasse to the townspeople who waited to grab hold, creating a safety net over the fiery chasm. And Sam landed safely, with a few grunts and groans from his living blanket.

Relief coursing through him, Will reached over the blanket and grabbed Sam, pulled him to the edge, and gave him a bear hug.

The musketeers pulled back the living blanket of Kiggles that saved Sam from the fires below, and the Kiggles let go of each other, chattering happily over the success of their plan.

Stitch said, "I told you we Kiggles would come in handy someday, didn't I?"

Smiling, Will put his finger out and Stitch put his hand on it.

Then Will drew his sword and yelled at the mist, "I will never give in!"

Jules did the same. "I will never bow to you!"

Arrie drew his sword as Porty shrugged and did the same. "You will never get us to submit!"

Tivona, Leata, David, Saul, Solomon, Joshua, Troddie, and Jess all did the same, and, one by one, the soldiers and townspeople who had fought so hard to defeat the dark enemy yelled, "We will never give in! We trust our Giver!" As the chants grew louder and louder, the dark mist dissipated until it disappeared. The crowd erupted in a roaring cheer, and the sun broke through to brighten their faces.

David took Will's arm and raised it, eliciting another series of cheers from the people of the newly united kingdom. Will smiled as he brought Sam to their father, who was just regaining consciousness. "Are you okay, Dad?"

Willy rubbed the back of his head. "Will, are you all right? What happened? Where's Sam?"

"We're good. I want to introduce you to someone." Will guided Sam to the front. "Meet your youngest son."

Neither said a word as they locked eyes upon one another. Then, Willy opened his arms wide and pulled Sam in for a tight embrace.

"I *really* have a dad!" said Sam.

A peal of laughter and cheers revealed Sam had endeared himself to the crowd.

Willy climbed to his feet and put his arms around Will and Sam. "I'm sorry for not being there for so many years, but I couldn't be prouder of my sons. I mean that with every fiber of my being. I love you both."

Sam peered up at the face of the father he had never seen except for in the photo he'd held almost every day of his life. "I can't wait to show you to my mom and Poppie."

Will's expression dropped.

Jules said, "What is it, Will? Aren't you happy to have your family back?"

Will replied, "Sure, but without the pouch or knowing how to find the portal that can take us back, we may never see Mom and Poppie, and you guys may never see your families either."

Jules tapped one hand against the other. "We can't give up now. We've been through too much together."

Arrie stepped up. "She's right. The pouch must be here somewhere, and finding the portal should be a piece of cake after nearly being killed, attacked, and threatened."

Will felt a tug on his trouser leg and found Stitch at his

feet. "From now on, I have to remember to look down before I walk. What is it, Stitch?"

Stitch waved him over to the stone where he and the Kiggles had hidden for safety. The pouch lay behind it! Maybe it had fallen from him in the battle. Good thing it landed there.

Will picked it up, the pouch that had guided and safeguarded him and his companions for their entire journey. Inside, he found the leather-bound book and the goblet with a number *2* on its pewter bowl. He opened the book in hopes of a new message.

On the last page were the words: *You have shown courage, love, loyalty, trust, and willingness to sacrifice even your own life for others. We are well pleased and proud of you, and you should be as well. Well done, Will Donovan.*

Chapter 34

Will stood in the square, gazing at the words in the book.

His father asked, "What is it, Will? Are you okay?"

Will shook off his trance and closed the book. "Oh, it's nothing. We still need to find the portal, or we'll be stuck here like you've been for ten years."

Willy nodded. "Will, not having each other for the past ten years has been a great sacrifice to you, Sam, and me, but maybe there was a purpose, a plan for why that had to be. This kingdom might have been destroyed without your journey to find Sam. I truly believe that you were that plan, and that's why the Taker was so focused on you all along. He thought he saw a selfishness in you, but he found a young man who was anything but selfish. I believe we will find the portal and get back home."

Will nodded. "I don't want Mom to be alone and lose us too."

Willy rubbed his sons's hair, smiling. "We won't give up until we find our way back. In the meantime, let's help put the town back to rights."

The bodies of the beasts and enemy creatures had turned into dust, but there was still a lot of work to be done.

"We appreciate your help restoring the city, but we know you desire to return to your home and family," said David. "Are you sure the portal is in Philidopheos?"

Will replied, "That's what we were told. I can't say for sure, but we have no other clues as to where it might be."

An old beggar nearby let out a groan as he lowered

himself onto a rock to sit.

David approached him. "Old man, are you feeling well? What is your name?"

"My name makes no difference." The old man pulled the lapels of his tattered jacket together to cover up his dirty shirt. Then he gazed up, revealing a worn face with a patch over one eye.

David put his hand on the man's shoulder. It was possibly the first time anyone had touched him in years. "Well, it makes a difference to me. You seem to be on hard times. How can we help you?"

The old man groaned as David's hand remained on his shoulder. "My name is Jeremiah, but no one bothers to call me anything these days."

David patted his shoulder. "Jeremiah, from now on, every man in this new kingdom is my friend and, more than that, my brother."

Jeremiah huffed in disbelief. "My sins are too great."

"This day is a new start for everyone. How can I help you?" David smiled.

Jeremiah shook his head. "I overheard your conversation. I might be able to help the boy."

Their interests sparked, the friends gathered around. David asked, "How can you help Will?"

"You're looking for the passageway to another time, am I right?" asked the man.

Will nodded attentively.

"I have heard of such a passageway."

Will's eyes widened. "Can you show it to us?"

"It is in a place where no one would go. A tomb," the man said with a heavy breath.

David frowned, suspicion in his eyes. "A tomb? What tomb?"

"An empty tomb," the man said, "one that had been set aside for a new king in the city. Inside is a gilded box which holds answers for the king and your way home . . ."

David shook his head and turned to Will. When they glanced back, the old man had vanished. No one had seen him walk away.

Jules turned in a circle, looking all around them. "That was weird. Where would we find a tomb in Philidopheos?"

Will tightened his brow. "He said a tomb for a new king, right?"

Jules replied, "Yeah, and where would the king be found?"

They exchanged glances, both smiling, and said together, "In the palace!"

Sam murmured, "Or under the palace."

"Under?" Will cocked his head.

"Don't they bury people underground? Plus, I saw something under the palace that looked like those Egyptian tombs at the museum Poppie took us to."

David interjected, "Actually, that makes a lot of sense."

Sam stood a bit taller at the compliment and headed toward the opening.

They re-entered the underground tunnel network and followed the corridors until they reached the jail cells from which they'd freed Saul, David, and Willy.

Sam pointed down another darkened passageway as David grabbed a torch to light the way. "I got lost when I tried to follow the Kiggles down here. See the gold around the opening?"

A little further, they came to a series of ornate tomb doors decorated with colorful paintings and etchings. Each was sealed shut. At the end of the corridor stood a golden door lit from above. David approached the door and knelt before it.

Tivona gasped.

As soon as David knelt, a series of short metal-tipped arrows shot across the corridor directly over his head, none of them touching David. Unperturbed, he stood and pushed the gold door inward.

Saul bowed his head slightly. "Only a humble man would be chosen king for the new kingdom."

A gilded chest the size of a large travel trunk sat inside the tomb. Will scanned the tomb but saw nothing else. David, Saul, Solomon, and Willy lifted the heavy box and carried it to the palace and the marble landing outside the main doors. The citizens of Philidopheos stood there, joined by soldiers from the other six cities in the kingdom. Once word spread, everyone became curious about the gold-decorated container at the palace entrance.

Will watched as David gazed out at the palace square ravaged from battle. His eyes rose from the broken city to his people's faces, and he smiled. The gathering crowd returned the gaze, anticipation in their eyes.

Their new king and leader would begin a new era of peace and unity. Tivona stood at his side with Leata and Saul. David smiled at his new faithful friends who stood across from them: Troddie, Jess, Solomon, Beno, Porty, Arrie, Jules, Willy, Sam, and finally, Will, to whom he gave a special nod.

Will returned the nod with a grin.

"People of Lydia, Eppita, Sumara, Perggia, Thytira, Sidar, and Philidopheos, we are now one kingdom, not because we were indecisive or selfish, but because we made a choice and fought for what was right, good, and true. I have no doubt that the Taker will try again to divide us, to plant seeds of doubt and divisiveness, to appeal to our weaknesses, but I have faith and trust in our strength and resolve to never go back to where we've been, to the barren wasteland that was our land and in our hearts. We have the blessing, wisdom, and strength from the Giver, who is with us always—we just need to trust that in our hearts every day. Will Donovan has taught me how possible that is.

"Tivona shared with me his story. How he and his friends, Jules, Arrie, and Porty, risked their lives to find Will's younger brother, Sam. Along the way, he discovered that our kingdom always had people who were courageous, loyal, honest, and selfless. Tivona and Leata risked their lives to journey with them. Then Stephen and Solomon also knew the right thing to do. I would like to dedicate this day to Stephen, who gave the greatest gift a friend could ever give to another, his very life."

There was a moment of silence in recognition of Stephen's sacrifice.

"We also honor Joshua for raising such a son of honor and selflessness." David bowed with respect to Joshua who returned the bow.

"Jess and Troddie did not hesitate to risk their lives for their friends and this kingdom. We honor your leadership and example as well. I don't want to forget Beno and the Lydian soldiers who arrived along with all the brave soldiers from Eppita, Sumara, Perggia, Thytira, and Sidar to support what appeared to be a hopeless battle for the citizens of Philidopheos. We could not have done it alone." Then David waved Stitch, his family, and the other Kiggles forward. "I am offering full citizenship to Stitch and all the Kiggles if they accept. They showed incredible loyalty and courage as well. Sam would not be with us today without their help."

Sam stepped over to the Kiggles, squatted down, and offered his hand to Stitch.

David continued. "I survived my years of imprisonment because the men held captive with me became my dearest friends, and I honor them today, especially Tivona's father, Saul, and Will's dad. They deserve the best cheer you have."

A roar came from the crowd. As it subsided, David turned to Will and grabbed his shoulder. "Lastly, I want to recognize a hero and friend of the kingdom." He withdrew a medal hanging from a brightly colored ribbon, which he eased over Will's head. "Without Will, our victory and our seven separate cities becoming one great kingdom again would not have happened. Few young men his age would have persevered in the face of direct attacks from the deceitful Taker. Will trusted in the good, put his brother's life ahead of his own, and inspired us to rally around a single cause—a cause of good."

David lifted Will's arm, and the crowd erupted into a loud cheer.

Will glanced at his proud father, smiling brother, and musketeer friends. Now, he knew the true meaning of friendship, love, trust, and courage. Feeling a bit undeserving of the attention, a sense of warmth washed over him. He waved over his family and friends and draped the medal around Sam's neck.

David approached the gilded container. "I know you are all as curious as I am to see what is in this golden box." Everyone stood on their toes and leaned forward as he opened the heavy lid. A bright glowing light emitted from the trunk as it opened. A rolled-up scroll lay atop golden objects inside.

The sun shone on David's face as he lifted the scroll. On the outside, it read, *Only he who has been chosen to be the new king is worthy of opening this scroll.* David paused, unrolled it, and read the proclamation: an agreement between the Giver and the new kingdom. Written in elegant language, the message in the scroll explained that the Giver would never give up on the loyal people of the new kingdom and would protect them against deceitful forces that would continue to tempt them to break this covenant.

David looked at the golden objects inside the trunk but made no move to touch them: a golden crown for the new king and one with twelve stars for the queen.

The crowd cheered, "David! David! Hail to the king."

Saul stepped forward, picked up the gold crown, and placed it upon David's head as the crowd repeated the chant.

Jules exclaimed, "That other crown must be for Tivona. I saw an image of twelve stars above her head on the battlefield."

David whispered something to Saul, who nodded with a smile. Then he lifted the crown with twelve diamonds like stars around it and knelt before Tivona. "Would the fairest and bravest woman I have known and have never stopped loving accept my hand in marriage and honor us all by being our queen?"

Tivona let go of years of tears as she smiled and nodded. "Without hesitation, yes to both! I love you." She wrapped her arms around him, and they held a kiss that seemed like it would never end.

Saul shook David's hand, and David placed the crown on Tivona's head.

"Long live the queen!" roared the crowd.

David turned to Will and his companions. "Now, we must get you all home. We just need to figure out how."

"The old man said we would find the portal in the empty tomb. This chest was the only thing in that room, so I think the answer may be the chest itself," said Will.

David stared down into the empty chest. "You may be right, Will. Why would I ever doubt you?"

Will blinked a few times to make sure he saw it correctly. It seemed to have no bottom but went down into darkness like a tunnel.

Will removed the goblet from his pouch, finding the number *2* etched on the outside. "Luckily, we have two wishes left to make it back home."

His father said, "Will, you need to lead the way. I trust you are still being looked after."

Will struggled with the thought. "I need to make sure Sam gets back."

His father smiled at his son. "You will, but you need to lead."

Glancing at his brother, Will nodded in agreement. He said goodbye to David and Tivona and wished them the best in their life together. He said goodbye to Saul, Solomon, and Troddie and thanked them for everything they did. He smiled at Leata, knowing he would miss her, but also because she held Jess's hand.

With a tear running down her face, she leaned over and kissed his cheek.

Will squatted to address his shorter friends. "Beno. You didn't forget me, and I'll never forget you and your fellow Lydians." Will reached down and picked up Stitch. "What will I do without you, Stitch?"

Stitch choked up, saying, "I think you've already proven that. You helped me find my family and my people. We will have a good life here now, but I'm available anytime you need me."

Will reached out his finger, and Stitch put his tiny hand on it to say goodbye.

Finally, Will turned to his family and friends and took a big breath. "I hope this works. I'll go first, and then each of you will follow. Okay?" Before he could jump into the gilded chest, Jules rushed toward him and—apparently not taking any chances... in case anything went wrong and they never saw each other again—she kissed Will squarely on the lips.

Arrie and Porty exchanged surprised glances, and Will's cheeks burned hotter than ever as he waved to the crowd, thanking them and wishing them the best.

Then, Will held the goblet out and said, "I wish for Porty, Arrie, Jules, Sam, my dad, and myself to travel home safely through this portal." With a "One, two, three," he jumped into the gilded chest.

Chapter 35

Will spiraled downward faster and faster through a dark, empty tunnel. Before he knew it, he hit a wooden floor with a loud thud—the attic floor! Anyone downstairs likely heard him. He jumped up and spun around several times, appreciating every detail of his cozy old attic. Pieces of candy still lay on the rug, the hanging light swung gently and threw shadows on the wall, and all his fondest memories hung on the walls of this place he loved and happily shared with his best friends.

His gaze shifting to the picture of The Three Musketeers on the wall, he laughed. But then he stopped and turned to the back wall. No one else followed him through the portal. He was alone.

He pulled the goblet from the pouch. How should he word the last wish to get them back? Before he could think, a shuffling came from near the attic door. The door opened, and there stood his grandfather, huffing and puffing after climbing the two flights of steep stairs to the attic of their old Victorian home.

"Poppie!"

Poppie made the final two steps into the attic, a broad smile stretching across his face as he gazed at Will. Will hugged him as Poppie said, "You made it back. Were you successful in your journey? You'll have to tell me all about it."

He hugged his grandfather and then stepped back. "Poppie, the others haven't followed me through the portal. Did I need a wish for each one of them? Did I use them up, and now they are lost forever?"

Poppie chuckled and continued to breathe deeply to catch his breath. "Maybe I should sit. I think the climb made me dizzy. Did you find Sam?"

"Yes, and—"

As Poppie leaned on the chair, he lost his balance and fell to the floor.

"Poppie!" Will blurted in a hushed voice, not wanting his mother to hear him. He dropped to his knees and put his arms around his grandfather. "Poppie, are you okay?"

Poppie made no response; he just lay awkwardly on his side.

Will tried to roll him onto his back. His grandfather was not breathing. Was it due to his heart condition? He'd survived one heart attack when Will and Sam were very small.

Panic and pain shot through Will's heart. "No, no, no, Poppie, you can't go. I need you. Dad, your son, is alive and coming to see you! You have to see him, Poppie!"

Tears streamed down Will's face onto his grandfather's tweed jacket, and he could feel the damp material on his cheek. His body shook at the thought of losing his grandfather, the man who loved him unconditionally and who he could trust with anything. Will turned to breathe in the familiar scent of his grandfather's jacket, with its hint of cigar smell that had always comforted him. He glimpsed the goblet on the ground and the number *1* now etched on it. He reached out and grabbed it, conflicted. Could he wish his grandfather back to life? If he did, would Sam, his father, and friends be lost forever in another time?

Clashing thoughts raced through his head as he held the grandfather he loved, but the loudest voice in his head kept saying, *Trust your instincts, Will.* Deciding to act instead of think, he closed his eyes and said, "I wish for my grandfather to be back with us and meet his son again." When he opened his eyes, a thud came from behind.

"That was cool," Sam said as Will turned around.

"Sam!" Will threw his arms around his brother.

Sam hugged him back and then pushed away. "Hey, why is Poppie on the floor?"

Poppie raised his head and smiled. "Haven't you ever seen anyone playing dead before? Sam, how was your adventure?" Poppie glanced at the goblet.

Will looked, too, finding the number *0* now on its face.

Poppie tilted his head as he glanced up at Will and squinted momentarily.

Sam's eyes widened. "It was crazy, scary, and amazing. Better than trick-or-treating."

Poppie slowly sat up and laughed.

"And guess what?" added Sam.

"What's that, young adventurer?"

"We have a treat for you." Sam's eyes gleamed.

Just then, another thud came from somewhere in the shadows, followed by another, and then a third that was louder than the others. Jules, Arrie, and Porty made their return to the attic!

Will wanted to cheer, shout, and hug each of them.

"That chest was a little tight to get through." Porty rubbed his shoulder.

Jules and Arrie laughed.

Sam continued to scan the shadows in the attic, likely waiting for their father to return, but no one else appeared.

"What is it, Sam? Are you waiting for my treat?" asked

Poppie.

Sam continued waiting and watching.

Will touched Poppie's shoulder. "Are you okay?"

"Never felt better," replied Poppie. "What did you do with that last wish?"

Will smiled. Poppie must've suspected something. "Poppie, I have something important to tell you."

Before he could continue, Mom's voice came from downstairs. "What's going on up there? What's banging around? I never knew that counting candy could be such a noisy business."

Will nervously darted to the doorway. "Everything's fine, Mom!"

Before he turned back to the others, another thud made him jump.

"And what was that?" she shouted again.

"Nothing, Mom. We'll be down soon."

"Good. I have some pumpkin and apple pies if anyone is interested!"

Will turned.

A tear ran down Poppie's cheek as he gazed upon his son after ten long years of wondering about his fate.

Will felt an incredible sense of well-being as he watched his father and grandfather embrace with genuine affection and love. This moment made all the trials and difficulties of his journey worth it.

After everyone greeted each other, they pounded down the stairs: Sam, Will, Poppie, Jules, Arrie, and Porty.

Porty enthusiastically asked, "Was there some offer for pie, Mrs. Donovan?"

"There certainly is. I'm sure all the trick-or-treating for you musketeers and the mummy built up an appetite."

"You'd be very surprised," replied Jules, sitting at the

kitchen table.

"Porty, would you like apple or pumpkin?"

"Yes, please." Porty nodded, so she put two pieces of pie on his plate.

As they all sat down at the table with their pie, Will waved to Sam. "Sam, come sit beside me. I think your costume looked really authentic tonight. We should start planning next year's if you want to go together."

Mom's eyes widened with surprise. She leaned toward Poppie and whispered, "Did you put something in their Snickers bars?"

Poppie laughed out loud. "Just two brothers appreciating precious time together. We do have a surprise for you, though. Don't we, boys?"

Will and Sam smiled at each other. Everyone else smiled and exchanged glances too.

Mom squinted with suspicion. "What's going on here? All that commotion in the attic and now this. Are you about to play a trick on me?"

Will stood and took Mom's shoulder. "More like a treat, actually, for all of us." He stepped into the hallway and brought his father into the kitchen.

Mom stood speechless, eyes wide and hand to her chest. Poppie shuffled to her as she opened her mouth as if trying to speak. Then her eyes closed, and she swooned. Poppie caught her, seeming to predict she'd have that reaction.

Willy raced over and took his wife in his arms.

Mom opened her eyes again, tears welling in them. "Willy? Is it really you? How . . . ?"

Smiling broadly, Willy put his forefinger to her lips. "Shhhh. It's really me. I'm here, and I've been waiting for this moment for a very long time." Wrapping his arms around her, he kissed her. "It's a very long story, but being home with my family is all that matters right now."

Will and Sam joined the hug as Mom continued to shake her head.

Jules finished her pie and got up. "We'll head home now so you guys can catch up."

Arrie stood up to join her while Porty shoved in two more forkfuls of pie.

Will joined the other Three Musketeers at the door. "Hey, I can't thank you guys enough for being there for me."

"All for one, Will." Arrie smiled. "Enjoy your family."

Porty leaned in. "You deserve it, but we are coming back for our candy."

Will laughed and patted Porty on the back as they left by the kitchen door. As they reached the sidewalk, Will called out from the doorway, "Hey, Jules. Would you be interested in seeing a movie or something sometime?"

A smile flashed over her face, and she nodded.

As Will closed the door, he caught his grandfather watching him. While time had not changed, Poppie seemed to know something in Will had changed. He had grown in many ways from the gifts of the journey, and Will could feel it too.

The End

About the Author

Award-winning author, Jim Sano, grew up in an Irish/Italian family in Massachusetts. Jim is a husband, father, lifelong Catholic, and has worked as a teacher, consultant, and businessman. He has degrees from Boston College and Bentley University and is currently attending Franciscan University for a master's degree in Catechetics and Evangelization. He has also attended certificate programs at The Theological Institute for the New Evangelization at St. John's Seminary and the Apologetics Academy. Jim is a member of the Catholic Writers Guild and has enjoyed growing in his faith and now sharing it through writing novels. *The Journey* is his seventh novel.

Jim resides in Medfield, Massachusetts, with his wife, Joanne, and has two daughters, Emily and Megan.

Published by
Full Quiver Publishing
PO Box 244
Pakenham, ON K0A2X0
Canada
www.fullquiverpublishing.com

www.ingramcontent.com/pod-product-compliance
Lightning Source LLC
Chambersburg PA
CBHW030135010826
48973CB00002B/566

* 9 7 8 1 9 8 7 9 7 0 6 9 2 *